Purpose

Fate Series

Book Two

By Deanna Harvey

RoseDog Books
PITTSBURGH, PENNSYLVANIA 15238

RoseDog Books
585 Alpha Drive
Suite 103
Pittsburgh, PA 15238
Visit our website at www.rosedogbookstore.com

ISBN: 979-8-88812-353-9
eISBN: 979-8-88812-853-4

Chapter One

Amelia

I walk outside and sit on the porch swing with my cup of coffee. I love the feeling of the warm glass on my hand and the sweet smell of french vanilla. The morning air is cool, the grass is covered in dew, and the sun is starting to rise. I love watching the sunrise in the morning while I wait for Colin to wake up.

As I sit quietly, I can't stop myself from thinking about the day we battled the serpents. It was about six months ago. Although, it feels as if it were just yesterday.

Right after the force field came down I told Colin that I needed to check on my grandfather but I also needed to find Stella. He said, "I'll check on your grandfather while you find Stella. I am so proud of you, but please be careful. I just got you back."

I kissed him and said, "I will always come back to you. I love you." He pulled my face into his like it was life or death. He kissed me with so much passion and need that it almost took my breath. Then he left me as he ran to check on my Grandfather.

I went out the back door and was immediately attacked by a serpent with long purple hair. She had golden brown eyes and she wore really dark makeup

My heart burst in my chest the moment my eyes met hers. I

don't know what it was but just looking at her made my head hurt.

I winced in pain as I grabbed my head.

"You'll be easy to kill", she said cackling in a high pitched laugh. There was something sadistic and scary about the look in her eyes.

I didn't say a word, I just hit her with everything I had. She didn't act like I hit her at all. Every time she smiled I would hit her even harder. Every spell more powerful than the last.

I was giving her everything I had.

In the middle of the battle with her I started to get tired. Sweat dripped down my face, my hands were trembling, and I could hear myself breathing heavily. Flashes of my parents smiling, laughing, and singing to me came across my mind. Visions of Colin and I dancing in the flower field brought tears to my eyes. All I could think about was making it out of the fight to get back to them.

The girl had gotten a few really good hits. One on my shoulder, one on my stomach, and lastly one on my knee. I wanted to fall to the ground from the agonizing pain.

Thankfully I was saved by a man that had a lot of tattoos. I was scared at first, because I thought he was a serpent when he approached us. But then he started helping me.

Her eye contact quickly went from me to him.

She kept taunting us and laughing. Her spells were effortless. She was having fun watching us try to beat her.

The harder we tried the more amused she got.

Her laugh pierced my ears. She started to get distracted by the man that was helping me. She was almost flirting with him as she fought with him.

He didn't say a word to her though. They just kept staring right into eachothers eyes while they fought.

Unfortunately right as I thought we were about to defeat her, she did a spell to cover all of us in a big cloud of smoke and then vanished into thin air.

I knew we almost had her. She was good at pretending that our spells did not phase her.

The man's name that helped me was Jack. He is Colin's friend. He also told me that the serpent girl's name is Mia. He had fought alongside her when he was still a part of the serpents. Jack said that she is ruthless and evil. Mia does not care for anyone. Not humans, witches, or even her fellow serpents. They look around the same age.

I asked him why she was flirting with him and he said that she does that with everyone. But the look on his face told a different story.

As Jack and I were healing our wounds Colin, a woman, and a man came running up to us. Colin introduced them. The woman's name was Amber and the man's name was Ace. We didn't really have time to talk. We had to go around helping my family fight the rest of the serpents that were still there.

The worst part of the battle that day was finding Stella in the forest behind the house with a group of Serpents attacking her. She was trying her best to hold them off, but she couldn't do it on her own.

Colin, Ace, Amber, and I took all of them out one by one. The moment they were all down Stella fell to the ground.

I swear I felt the sound of the crackles of the leaves and the thud of her hitting the ground in my soul.

Colin picked her up as fast as he could and carried her to my parents room, while Amber and Ace guarded us on the way there.

It was like we were running in slow motion. I couldn't speak, breathe, or think.

I started trying to heal her the moment Colin laid her on the bed. I tried so hard to stop myself from crying but I couldn't. All I could keep thinking was why she was in the forest alone in the first place.

I stroked her strawberry blonde hair as tears fell down my face. Using my other hand I wrapped my pinky around hers and said, "You have to be okay. You promised me you would always be here for me. You can't be if you are not here."

Right as I stabilized Stella her parents came in. Their faces were pitiful. I felt their pain as they clinged to Stella.

I didn't want to leave her, but I had to go with Colin to go check inside and outside the house to make sure that there was no one else in the forest that needed help.

Everyone was either inside the house or outside the house fighting, all except my Grandmother.

The horrible feeling that washed over me had me sprinting out of the house and into the forest. I hoped I was not right but I feared the worst. Colin ran after me. I could feel his confusion. As I was running I said to him, "that's why Stella was in the forest. She must have seen my Grandmother go in here." Colin yelled back to Jack to tell him to let my family know, to keep fighting, and to tell Blaze to meet us in the forest.

The grass was dry. I could hear it crunching beneath my feet. Colin was running right by my side. The more we ran the worse I felt.

My stomach started to hurt and the nauseating feeling I had made me want to puke. It was like my brain was telling me to keep running but my body was fighting against me. Like my body was telling me it was a bad idea to keep going.

Right as I started to hear voices Blaze caught up to us. "Wait! I need to cast a spell on us so that way they dont sense us coming!"Blaze said with urgency as he casted the spell.

We stopped running and started to walk quietly. After a few minutes we could see my grandmother talking to a big man. We hid behind a tree so that way they couldn't see us. The man had a black robe on. His hood was up so we couldn't see his face.

My Grandmother didn't look afraid. She looked defiant and strong. I scooted a little closer to hear better. Blaze grabbed my hand and put his finger on his mouth to tell me to be quiet.

He whispered, "That is Ethan. He is the leader of the serpents. If he finds out that Colin is the son of Joseph and Kate he will immediately kill him. They killed Adam, his son. He found out that I was Joseph's brother the day that I made a scene in front of everyone. Colin and I are doomed if he sees us."

My stomach that was already in knots hurt even more. The

thought of something going wrong made me dizzy.

"I see that you got my message.", Ethan said, taunting my grandmother.

"I am here because I want this all to stop. Not because I am afraid of you. Colin has done nothing to you. His parents' doings are not his. You need to leave him alone" my Grandmother said. Her bravery made me smile.

"They took my son from me. It is only fair that I take theirs. All this will stop if you just hand him over to me. I will never bother your family again." Ethan said, his voice got so serious.

I could hear his tolerance wavering at my grandmother's lack of compliance.

"Colin is a part of my family now. I will not hand him over. I will not let any harm come to him." My grandmother said in a very defensive tone.

Right as Ethan was about to respond I lost my balance and fell. I crashed to the ground. I could feel the sticks and leaves beneath me snapping and breaking. It was like the volume around me was turned all the way up. Everything sounded so loud even the sound of my heart beating in my chest.

I have never felt so much fear in my life. My whole body started to shake. I was sure that I was going to get sick at any moment.

When I looked up I could see the panic on my grandmother's face. Colin and Blaze rushed to my side. I pushed them away and told them to run, but they didn't budge. Colin put his arm around me and held me close. I could feel his protectiveness like a cloak draped around me. Blaze stood in front of us, daring Ethan to move even an inch toward us. He pulled his wand out ready to fight.

"It's been a long time, Blaze.", Ethan said, taunting him.

"Leave them out of this Ethan. They're just kids. They've done nothing to you.", Blaze said his words were filled with anger.

Ethan started to walk slowly toward us. He still hadn't pulled out his wand. I know he doesn't even need his wand. He took off his hood. His eyes were so dark that they almost looked black. He had long grayish black hair. You could see the evil in his face. He grinned at us as he walked toward us.

I could tell that he was not fazed by Blaze's presence at all.

All the fear I had vanished. No one can defeat him. I did not care what happened to me. I had to save Colin.

I pulled away from Colin. He went to pull me back but I pushed his hand away. I looked into his eyes. I could feel the tears falling down my face.

"He'll have to go through me. I won't let him hurt you. I can't lose you again. I love you" I screamed, my voice breaking.

I could feel his hand shaking as he pulled me in to kiss me. His lips trembled against mine as we embraced each other.

"So the boy has fallen in love with your Granddaughter. This is why you are so protective over him. Nothing good comes from falling in love. Isn't that right Elenor?" Ethan said laughing.

My grandmother pulled out her wand. "LEAVE THEM ALONE", she said, her voice booming throughout the forest. The ground shook and jolted Colin and I apart. Even Blaze seemed startled.

"How dare you challenge me?! How dare you speak to me in that tone! You really think that you could hurt me? You above all people should know better than that Elenor. Noone challenges me and lives to tell the tale." Ethan yelled at my grandmother. His eyes somehow got even darker. He started to rise off the ground. Magic started to come out of his hands like small rays of lightning.

Somehow my grandmother didn't even flinch. Not even a hint of fear showed on her face.

But before he or any of us could make a move, Ace and a bunch of my family members ran toward us.

Ethan shifted out of the forest before any of us could do anything.

I ran to my grandmother and hugged her very tight. After a moment Colin approached us. "Thank you for taking up for me and saying that I am a part of your family.", Colin said with sadness in his voice.

"Of course you are a part of our family. It doesn't take someone with magic to feel the connection you two have.", my grandmother said smiling, pulling us both in for a hug.

But the smile was only there for a moment before she let go of us and told us that we would have to leave. Ethan was going to come looking for Colin and Blaze. So we needed to go into hiding.

We all walked back to the house together. Colin held my hand as we walked. He stoked each one of my fingers with each step that we took.

I felt my heart beat slow down and my breathing come back to normal as we reached the house. He could sense it as he looked down at me. I met his gaze and smiled with the look of relief on his face. His eyes said "I love you" so I squeezed his hand, saying "I love you too"

When we got back to the house all of the serpents were gone. Carol and Beth were going around healing anyone that was wounded while everyone else helped my mother clean up.

Blaze and Amber were going around turning the serpents into ash that were dead. When Amber got to Liam, Blaze stopped her. "I should hate him. A part of me does. But he was the only best friend I had growing up. To me he was the only person that didn't think I was nothing. He deserved his fate. But none of us can forget that we could have been him. We could have died fighting on the wrong side. We escaped the serpents. Some people never get the chance too.", Blaze said, looking at Amber, Ace, and Jack. He lifted his wand, his hand shaking, then he put his head down as he casted the spell, turning Liam into Ash. Blaze slowly lifted his head as he watched Liam's ashes disappear into the wind.

We all watched in silence for a moment. It was like a switch went on after a minute or two. Blaze just walked away and began to help again. I think it is a gift and a curse the way he can turn his emotions on and off. I want so badly for him to have a happy life one day. He deserves it.

I went upstairs to check on Stella. She was awake laying on the bed. I ran to her and hugged her. I could feel how weak she was as she could barely hug me back. "Grandmother is okay. But Ethan, the leader of the serpents, is out to get Colin and Blaze. I have to leave with Colin. I cannot be away from him again. I just can't. I thought I had lost you. I don't know if I would have made it through it.``, I said to Stella quietly.

"I felt her presence while I was fighting. I turned around and it was like time stopped for a moment. I could see her going into the forest. But no one else noticed her but me. I finished off the person I was fighting but by the time I went in she was too far. Then some of the serpents followed me in and I was out numbered. I am going to miss you. But I understand. We will be together again soon. You and Colin need each other like the grass needs the rain. I would never want to watch you be separated from him again. I will think about you everyday.", Stella said as she put her head down.

I crawled into bed with her and gently laid my head on her chest. "I am going to miss you every single day until I can come back.", I said as tears swelled in my eyes.

"Promise you'll come back?"Stella asked, crying.

"I pinky promise. Forever, remember? You are my best friend.", I said, as I wrapped my pinky around hers.

"I love you. Please be careful.", Stella said. She tried to move her arm up so she could wrap her pinky around mine, but she winced in pain.

"Stop. Please rest. I love you too. I will. I will be back as soon as I can,"I said. Then I tucked Stella in and gave her a hug. I could feel the pain in my chest as I walked away and shut the door behind me.

I stood by the door for a brief moment. I felt like someone dropped a boulder on me. Like I was being crushed by pain. I did not want to leave Stella. But I knew I had to.

I went back down stairs. When my mother and father stopped and looked at me, they knew. They both knew that I had to leave. They wrapped their arms around Colin and I. My mothers body shook from crying as she hugged us. My father tried to be strong for all of us, but he couldn't hide the tears swelling up in his eyes.

I can still feel the unbearable pain I felt in my heart in that moment when I think about it.

Everyone but Sophia and her family decided to stay to protect my parents. Ace, Jack, and Amber decided to stay in Colins old house. Just in case any serpents came back. Blaze left that night to gather more people.

Before he left he took Colin outside and talked to him for a while. I could tell that they had grown very close. When they got back in he told Colin and I that he owned a cabin in a rural part of Kentucky where we would be safe to hide out in.

My mother made a big meal that night for everyone. After dinner my mother and father took me outside. They told me to be careful, how much they loved me, and to come back home as soon as I could. I held them both for a long time. They hugged me and kissed me before letting go. Before they went back in I told them to have Colin meet me in the tree treehouse.

Colin met me in the tree house. He was wearing a white t-shirt, a navy blue jacket, blue jeans, and his boots. I loved how his hair was combed over perfectly.

He came and sat next to me. I leaned over and laid my head on his chest. He put his arm around me, pulled me close, and started to nervously play with my hair.

"I'm so sorry that we have to leave. I know Seth and Grace understand, but still. I know you are going to miss them so much. I will too. I just feel so guilty for everything that is happening and pulling all of your family into this mess.", Colin said with his head down.

I sat up and looked Colin in the eyes as I said, "Stop. My family came to help us because they wanted to. They love you. I love you. You are a part of our family. You always have been. My grandmother can feel how much I love you and how much you love me. You are my home. As long as you are by my side I will be okay. One day when all of this is over we will be with my parents again. But right now we have to hide until we are strong enough to defeat Ethan. That is our Purpose. To avenge your parents and everyone else that the serpents killed or hurt. They have terrorized familes for years. We will make sure that no other child has to grow up without their parents, that no other young witch gets trapped in their evil group, and that no other innocent people die by their hands. It is up to us, my family, and Blaze. We're all in this together. We have to believe that something good is going to come from all the pain that we have been through. We are the reason that our parents met. Why our fathers were best friends and why our mothers were best friends. It was fate for them to all meet. Joseph was meant to fall in love with Kate and my parents were meant to fall in love. So that way you would be born and I would be born. Then with your parents death came Blaze. Blaze would have never come to us if your parents hadn't died. My family would have never come if Blaze had not taken you away. You see? The pain and the things that break us all have a light at the end of the tunnel or reason for happening. We might not see it at the moment, but one day we will. All of these things were fate, waiting to happen, so that way we could realize our purpose and what we are meant to do. "

It was quiet. I could tell he was really thinking about everything I said. I liked the pause in our conversation. It was just a few seconds but the wind felt nice and the cold wood from the treehouse felt good beneath me. Just being in there with Colin brought me so much peace.

"You are right. I will not stop until we defeat Ethan and every single one of his followers. I will not let my parents' death be in vain. I will not let all this pain be for nothing. Then we will come back home and have the life together that we have always dreamed of. I promise. I love you. Forever.", Colin said and then he tucked a piece of my hair behind my ear.

He scooted closer to me. Our noses were literally touching at that point. I could feel his warm breath on my face. He smelled like mint and the honey hand soap that my mother has in the kitchen. He looked so beautiful. Even with the dirt on his cheek and the tiredness that he had in his eyes from fighting.

He smiled as he closed his eyes and placed his lips on mine. Colin cupped my face with both of his hands. I parted my lips open for his tongue to glide across mine.

I felt warm, happy, and safe all the same time.

Our tongues danced and sparks flew. I loved the feeling of my hands in his hair and his hands on my face.

He pulled away just a little as he rested his forehead on mine. He dropped one hand to my hip and slowly caressed my cheek with his other hand. The moonlight shined down perfectly on us from the glass in the roof of the tree house.

It was magical.

I smile as I drank my coffee on the porch thinking about that kiss. Right as I sit my coffee back down, Shadow jumps onto my lap. Before Blaze left, he asked us to take Shadow with us. He didn't know how long he would be traveling to find people or the trouble that he would run into along the way. We dont mind. We love Shadow.

I miss my family so much. Colin has been so loving and kind since we arrived at the cabin. I do not know what I would do without him. He knows better than anyone how much I love my parents and how much I miss them.

We flew here on Colin's broom together. It felt like a dream being up in the sky with him. The stars were so beautiful that they didn't even look real. I held on to him so tight. At first I was scared and I wanted to close my eyes, but Colin told me to keep them open. Everything is so different at night when you're looking down at the world from the sky. It was like we were the only two people awake. I wanted it to last forever. Just him and I floating in the sky.

I know that Blaze can come back any time. Then we will have to leave to get ready to go fight the serpents again. At least we know that it will be the last time, because no matter what we are going to defeat them. Once and for all.

Chapter Two

Colin

I wake up and get a glass of water. I walk to the screen door and see Ameila sitting on the porch swing with Shadow. I love how her blonde curls fall perfectly around her face and that she looks so beautiful without even trying.

I crack open the screen door. She smiles at me and pats the spot next to her for me to come sit. Before I sit down next to her, I bend down letting my lips rest on hers for a few seconds, savoring the moment. I can feel her smile into our kiss then letting go as she says, "good morning".

"Good morning, love. I pet shadow and he purrs as he comes and sits on my lap. Amelia leans over and rests her head on my shoulder. "Are you okay?", I ask.

Amelia sits back up, smiles, and says, "I'm okay. I was just thinking about what our future is going to look like and how I can't wait to spend forever with you."

I can see the pink on her cheeks from her blushing. I sit Shadow down and pull Amelia on to my lap. I gently take each strand of her hair in her face and tuck it behind her ears slowly. I then move my hand from her hair to caress face. We embrace each other at the same time. Like our mouths are magnets to one another's and they cannot take a single moment longer being apart. Her lips are warm against mine. She wraps her arms around my neck and her legs around my waist. I pick her up and carry her into the living room.

When you first walk into the cabin there is the living room, there is a tan couch, a round coffee table with Amelia's books and my journal on it, and a basket next to the couch with a few blankets in it. There is a large window above the couch. You can see the beautiful forest and sky for miles. Next to the living room is the kitchen. There is a small table with two chairs. I love picking flowers for Amelia to put in the vase on the table like how my father did for my mother. There is a set of stairs next to the kitchen that lead to the upstairs loft. That's where Amelia and I sleep. The bathroom is also upstairs.

I lay Amelia on the couch. I can feel the heat between us. She tastes like sweet vanilla as I gently slide my tongue against hers. She runs her hand through my hair and I can hear her moan as I pull her closer against me.

She ignites a fire in me like gasoline.

I kiss from her lips, cheek, and down her neck.

I can feel her heartbeat racing against my chest. I can never get enough of her. I pull back enough just to give her a moment to stop and think.

"Do you want to stop?", I say, still holding on tight to her.

She breathes in nervously, "I just want our first time to be magical. I know it sounds silly, because I love you and I do want to.", Amelia says, putting her head down.

I raise Amelia's head up and kiss her softly. "Amelia, you do not have to explain yourself to me. If you are not ready right now we won't. I want you because I love you. I enjoy just being with you. It is okay. When the time comes we will both be ready. You won't be nervous. I could feel that you were. I don't want to ever make you nervous. I will make sure it is magical just the way you deserve it to be.", I say, then I place a single kiss on her cheek.

"Do you know how perfect you are Colin White?" Amelia says smiling.

I playfully kiss Amelia all over her face and pick her up off of the couch. "I will never be as perfect as you, my love. Nothing could ever be as perfect as you. Well not until we have a baby of our own, then something will be as perfect as you." I say as I rest my hand on her belly for a moment. Then I carry Amelia over to the kitchen and sit her on the counter.

"I can't wait to marry you and watch you be a father one day", Amelia says, smiling ear to ear.

"Whenever all this is over and we get to go home to be with your family, we can make that happen. But for now, do you want pancakes or french toast" I ask playfully.

"French toast please.", Ameila says giggling.

I make Amelia french toast and some orange juice. After we eat we decide to study. Amelia and I have still been training since we've been here. I miss Blaze and the others a lot sometimes. It's weird not training with them everyday. I know Amelia feels the same way about her family.

We have an area behind the cabin that we have been using to train. Amelia learned so much with her family. She got really close with her cousin Stella. She talks about her often. I can't wait to spend time with all of them.

Today Amelia and I are going to be defending ourselves against each other. It makes me nervous, because if I were to ever accidentally hurt Amelia I would never forgive myself. But she is stubborn. She also knows her abilities and how strong she is, so if I were to let her know that I was nervous about hurting her, she would get upset with me. So I just don't say anything and hope that I don't mess up. If I am being honest I am the one that could get hurt. Amelia's levitating skills are like nothing I've ever seen before. So I am probably the one that is going to get hurt.

I throw on a black tshirt, gray sweatpants, and then head outside.

Amelia meets me outside. She is wearing a white tank top, pink cotton shorts, no shoes, and her hair pulled back into a ponytail. I am trying so hard not to stare, because I do not want to be disrespectful. But it is hard, because Amelia looks breathtakingly gorgeous.

"Are you wearing that on purpose to distract me, love?" I say smirking at Amelia.

"I would never do such a thing.", Amelia says, winking at me.

Amelia and I take out our wands. She immediately lifts a log off of the ground and levitates it at me. I quickly cast a spell causing it to break into a bunch of pieces. Then I cast a spell at Amelia causing her to lose her balance. She regains her balance quickly and casts a fire spell at me. I then cast a spell to put it out before it gets anywhere near me. I then cast a water spell, soaking her to the bone.

"You did that on purpose!"Amelia says laughing.

"I plead the fifth.", I say, taunting her.

We go back and forth until the sun is about to set. The evening summer breeze is nice. Amelia and I walk around to the front of the cabin and up the steps. We sit on the porch swing together in silence for a few moments, taking in the beautiful sunset.

"I am going to go upstairs and shower before bed.", I say.

"Can I join you?" Amelia asks, smiling shyly.

"Of course you can, but are you sure you want to?", I ask.

"I am sure," Amelia answers. She kisses me and then walks inside. I grab a tshirt and a pair of shorts. Then I go into the bathroom and start the shower. Amelia comes in carrying a t-shirt, her underwear, and a couple towels for us. I have always thought that she looked the most beautiful without any makeup in her bed time clothes.

Amelia puts the stuff down and slowly gets undressed. Her cheeks are bright pink. I walk over to her and pull her into my arms. "If you want I can shower by myself. I promise it's okay.", I say.

Ameila kisses me and then looks into my eyes. "It's okay, I promise.", she says as she turns and gets into the shower. I get undressed and get into the shower. Amelia is perfect. She is petite but curvy at the same time. It kills me that she is self conscious about her body. I love her body and every single thing else about her. I would not change a thing.

Our parents never made a big deal about nudity and things like that. So Amelia and I being naked right now doesnt bother me. We never watched TV, all our schooling was done at home with our witch training, and all we have ever had was each other. I am more comfortable with Amelia than anyone else. Being naked in front of her is normal to me. Physically and emotionally.

Amelia gestures for me to come and stand under the water with her. I go under the water, pull her close to me, grab the shampoo, and turn her around. I put the shampoo on her head and I start lathering the soap into her hair. She leans her head back and I can feel my heart start beating faster. I start rubbing her head as I lather in the soap. She is just so beautiful. I lean down and kiss her neck. Then I rinse the soap out of her hair.

She turns around to face me. I can feel the air get caught in my throat. She pulls my face down gently to meet hers. She kisses me and I can feel her body getting closer and closer to mine until we are holding each other as close as possible.

I push us away from the water to put soap on her sponge. I look into her eyes as I run it along her body. I love how everything we experience together is a first for both of us. Everything we do together or to each other is strictly out of love and instinct.

I bend down as she puts soap in her hand so she can wash my hair for me and then I turn around so she can wash my back. After she gets done I turn around and pick her up to face me. She wraps her legs around me without hesitation. The water from the shower is pouring over us and the bathroom is hot from the steam. Little droplets of water run down her face and down her nose. I can barely breathe from how hot I am and how hot the bathroom is.

I feel like I could die from the desire, want, and need that I have for her. But I know we need to stop now before it goes any further.

I want to make this last kiss special. Our mouths meet with a rush of need and hunger for one another. Our tongues dance as our hands wander each other's bodies like a maze we've never been in.

I push her body up against the shower. The water is pouring over us. I love the sounds she makes, letting me know that our kiss bring her pleasure and that she is enjoying my hands exploring her body. I run my hand from her hip to her breast. I grip her hip with my other hand as she gasps into my mouth.

I taste her mouth one more time before removing my lips from hers and I whisper into her ear "I love you".

I gently sit her down. My body immediately aches for hers.

"I love you more", she says with a smile. I can see how flushed her face is from our time in the shower. I quickly get out, dry off, and get dressed. She turns off the water and then I help her out. I wrap her towel around her bottom half, then I pull her onto my lap as she faces away from me. I grab her lotion off of the counter and I start rubbing the lotion onto my hands. I massage her shoulders and back slowly.

I watch her face in the mirror. She looks up and notices me watching her. She has the cutest smile on her face. My heart leaps at seeing her this happy. It is intimate moments like this that make me fall even more in love with her.

I get more lotion off of the counter. Then I take some of the lotion and rub it on her arms and legs. I take my time feeling every inch of her body. The lotion helps my hands to glide effortlessly across her skin. I slowly graze my fingertips down her arm as I help pull her t-shirt over her head. I stop at her waist and let my hands stay there for just a moment before pulling her in for a kiss. Then I grab her brush and I begin to brush and braid her hair.

She goes to stand up but I pull her back into my lap,"I just want to hold you like this for a few more seconds.", I say but it comes out so quiet that I think she might not have heard me.

But her smile says otherwise. She lets me hold onto her waist and my head rests against hers. I listen to the sound of her breathing,

I memorize the rhythm of her heart beat, and I soak in the sweet smell of her hair.

My arms release her and she reluctantly stands up. Amelia goes downstairs to grab my journal off of the coffee table. I get into bed and take out my wand to put the stars on the ceiling. She climbs into bed and lays her head on my chest.

"You know sometimes I think that I could never love you any more than I already do, and then nights like tonight happen. You make me feel so beautiful, special, and loved.", Amelia says. I can hear the sincerity in her voice.

"All I have ever wanted to do is love you and make you happy. It is an honor to love you Amelia Jones. You deserve to be loved this way. Everyone does.", I say.

She wraps her arms around me and holds on as if I am going to disappear.

I cannot blame her for feeling that way. I kiss her sometimes like it will be the last time. I think we both fear being separated again more than we want to admit.

I pick up my book and I read to Amelia until she falls asleep with her head on my chest. I kiss her forehead and I close my eyes.

I meant what I said to her. Loving her is an honor. I smile as I drift off to sleep. I am so in love that it is like I am dreaming when I am awake. I cannot wait to wake up just to be with her again.

I wake up to the smell of coffee, bacon, and eggs. I walk downstairs and see Amelia cooking. Shadow is asleep in front of the screen door where the sun is coming in from outside.

"Good morning sleepy head", Amelia says as she comes over and kisses me. She goes back over to the counter and takes two pieces of toast out of the toaster. She sits our plates on the table and makes us both some coffee.

"Good morning my love. Thank you for making breakfast.", I say. We sit and eat together. Amelia reads her book as she eats.

"Let's go to the stream behind the cabin for a little while today." I say.

"That sounds fun. It can be like that lake that we went to with my parents." Amelia says, with joy in her voice.

I grab a bag. I pack a blanket, some snacks, a book for Amelia, and a couple towels. I come downstairs and see Amelia pouring some water into her cup. She is wearing a bikini and some jean shorts. She's not wearing makeup and her hair is in a messy bun. She looks breathtaking. I make eye contact with her and I realize I have been standing at the bottom of the stairs staring at her.

"I am sorry for staring. It's just, you look gorgeous today. You look beautiful everyday, but even more today." I stutter trying to get my words out.

Amelia walks over to me, stands on her tiptoes, wraps her arms around my neck, kisses me, smiles, and says thank you. I grab ahold of her hand, spin her back around to me, and kiss her again with so much passion that I even have to let go to catch my breath.

"What was that for", Amelia says, blushing.

"I just love you" I say, smiling. Then I go upstairs to get ready.

We walk down to the stream together. It is hot, but the breeze is nice. I pull out my wand and use a spell to unpack the bag. Amelia takes off her shoes and steps into the lake.

I take off my shoes and sit them next to Amelias. I get into the water. She stops splashing for a moment. I pull her close to me and kiss her. "I'm sorry love.", I say. She looks at with confusion on her face. Before she can say a word I pick her up and dunk her into the water. I start laughing hysterically. I can see the shock on her face as she rises out of the water. She starts laughing as she wipes the water off her face.

We both start splashing and trying to dunk each other. I love the way the water glistens in the sun and the sound of her laughter takes over. Not even the birds or the sound of the trees blowing compares to the beauty of her laugh.

I see goosebumps starting to form on Amelia's arms. I do not want her to be cold. I lead her out of the water and we lay on the blanket together. Amelia and I eat our snacks together that I packed. She pulls out her book and reads aloud as I play with her hair. Her silky curls effortlessly move through my fingers.

The sound of her voice reading, the wind blowing, and the water moving down the stream is so peaceful. I could stay here like this with her forever. By the time we get back to the cabin it's dinner time. Amelia's favorite food has always been grilled cheese and tomato soup.

After we get cleaned up and dry clothes on I start making it for her. While I cook Amelia lays on the couch, reading, and holding Shadow.

After we get done eating we use our magic to clean up the house. Once we get done we go upstairs and lay down.

"I had so much fun today.", Amelia says while she changes into night clothes. I throw on some shorts and climb into bed.

"I had fun today too. Especially throwing you into the water", I say laughing.

"Haha, really funny. You were only able to get me because I was distracted by kissing you.", Amelia says, rolling her eyes.

She climbs into bed while wearing a tank top with no bra and a pair of pantys. An animalistic growl escapes me as I sit up and flip Amelia onto the bed and climb on top of her. "Are you distracted now?" I ask, with a taunting tone.

Amelia is blushing and smiling so big. I kiss her all over her face and then her lips. "I love you so much", she says. Her eyes looking into mine like energy pulling my soul to hers. There are so many things I want to do and say to her. As she lays on the bed under me I cannot help but feel like my heart is going to beat out of my chest.

My lips are getting dryer and dryer each moment that passes as I stare at her in amazement. My mouth slightly opened, and my mind racing with thoughts of how much I want and desire her. I fantasize about her more and more each day. "I love you more", I say. WIthout letting my hunger and desperation take over I place my lips on hers. I kiss her slowly, taking my time to memorize the softness of her lips, the shape of them, and the taste of the mint from her toothpaste. I can barely contain myself as she clenches my shirt. I slide my hands under her shirt, place my hands on her hips.

I gently place her on to her side of the bed. I can feel my hands shaking against her body, "Would you like me to read to you?", I say, my voice sounding hoarse.

"I would love that.", Amelia says quietly. I get up and grab my journal.

I turn around to walk back to the bed. She is staring at me, I can see her trying to read me, and the questions running through her mind. I slowly walk back to the bed and sit down. "What is it love?", I say as I pull her close to me.

"Nothing, I just want to make sure you are okay?", she says.

"Amelia, I am fine. That was amazing. You are everything. Honestly I couldn't be happier.", I say, trying to reassure her. I see the worry in her eyes turn to joy and her beautiful smile return to her face.

I think everyone is born needing reassurance, compliments, and love. Some people just convince themselves that they don't need it.

I know that Amelia needs those things everyday. I do not mind. It brings her happiness. Real genuine happiness.

We both scoot down on the bed and I pull the covers over us as she lays her head onto my chest.

"What story do you want to hear tonight?", I ask.

"Read the one when your mom told your dad she was pregnant. It is one of my favorites.", She answers excitedly.

"Mine too", I say smiling.

I open my journal and turn to the page. "It was the beginning of September. My mother was ecstatic. Her and Grace both had a feeling they were pregnant. They both went to the doctor together. My mother was due in April and your mother was due with you in May. They immediately knew we were going to be best friends. My mother came home and made dinner for my father. She set the table with candles and their finest dishes. She made him his favorite dinner. Roast with carrots and potatoes. She put the flowers that he had picked her that morning in the vase in the middle of the table. It took her two hours to pick her dress. She said she wore a white sundress with her hair tied up into a ponytail with a white ribbon. Time stood still as my father walked through the front door. She had a million things that she planned to say. But when she looked into his eyes, he knew without her saying a word. He ran to her and fell to his knees crying tears of joy. He then stood up, lifted her off the ground, and spun around as they laughed and held each other. After dinner they spent the rest of night talking about baby names. When they told me the story when I was a little boy they both said it was the happiest day of their lives. I was going to be their greatest adventure."

Amelia looks up at me with tears in her eyes, "I miss them so much.", she says.

"I know. I miss them too.", I say then I kiss her forehead. I leave my lips there for a moment, before sucking in a breath. Talking about my parents brings me so much happiness but in the same breath it is the most excruciating pain. It is hard to not let the thought into my head that I'll never see them again and that all I have left is their stories. I can feel Amelia's body getting heavier. She is about to fall asleep. "I love you with every single fiber of my being. I don't know what I would do without you love.", I whisper into her ear.

"I love you more Colin.",she says in a sleepy voice. Her eyes get heavier and heavier until she falls asleep. She is so beautiful when she sleeps. I watch her chest going up and down slowly as she breathes. I gently rub her cheek. She smiles in her sleep.

I am overwhelmed with emotion as I lay here holding her. I am so in love with her, Sometimes I feel like my heart is going to burst when I look at her. I cannot wait for the day that we start a family of our own. I know that Amelia is right when she said that our purpose is to defeat the serpents. But she is and always will be my priority.

Nothing is more important to me than her and one day the family that we will build together.

Chapter Three

Amelia

The summer went by in a flash of Colin just being himself. Loving me, physically and emotionally. His devotion to my happiness and well being has always amazed me. I never had to ask for or deserve his love, it has always just been there. Like the air I breathe or my eyesight. I would be lost without it.

Fall has approached and I love how he soaks up every second.

I want to do something special for Colin. We turned eighteen back in April, but we decided not to celebrate until we were back home with everyone. I am going to set up a fire pit outside for us to do s'mores this evening. It will also give me a chance to use the fire spell that I've been working on.

I go to the closest to pick out some clothes. I get my khaki, white, and cream colored flannel, some light blue jeans, and my boots. I throw on some makeup and fix my hair. Colin is still asleep. I go downstairs and sit on the porch with Shadow.

Once the sun is completely up I go back inside and make omelets for us. He comes down stairs wearing some basketball shorts, his eyes still look sleepy, and his hair is growing out just enough for his hair to be in his eyes again. He is breathtaking.

I have always thought Colin was so handsome. I cannot imagine loving or being with anyone else. It feels like my soul was always meant to be with him. I think that's why we were born on the same day. We had to be together from the very beginning of our life. I know Colin and I are going to have a beautiful and long life together. I can feel it.

I know he doesn't like thinking about the future because he knows anything can happen. But I love thinking about the future, because I see him.

"You look beautiful" Colin says as he kisses me on the cheek before sitting down at the table.

"Thank you. I have to go to that corner store that is at the top of the hill once we get done eating. It's a surprise so you can't come with me.", I say then I wink at him.

"Oooh do I get a hint?"Colin asks, in an excited voice. He has always loved surprises and gifts. Joseph and Kate used to be the best at surprises and presents. They would go all out with decorations for holidays and birthdays. I miss it so much. I know Colin does too.

My mother and father have always said that the experience was a gift. Wherever we went or whatever we did on my birthday was worth more than any physical gift.

"Your surprise will be outside in the front yard this evening right before the sun goes down." I say.

I finish my food, give Colin a kiss, and start walking to the corner store. I really want to learn how to shift to different places like how Blaze and Ethan do. I have read the spell to do it a hundred times, but I know I am still not ready to do it yet. It takes a lot of practice and time to master and successfully do the spell.

The dirt road leading up to the main road is long. But watching the leaves fall around me is relaxing. It is crazy how much you enjoy things when someone that you care about loves it. You see it in a whole new light. At first I did not like the fall. I remember being like seven and not liking it because it meant that summer was over. That was until I saw the way Colin lit up when he would watch the leaves fall as he sat in our treehouse. He would just sit there in awe for hours. It made me see the beauty in the colors. Fall makes the world look like a painting.

The country store looks rustic on the outside. There are old men sitting in rocking chairs talking to each other outside. The old men smile and nod their heads at me as I walk into the store. I grab marshmallows, graham crackers, and chocolate. The lady at the checkout counter is really nice. Her name is Cathy. She is older. She has a really country accent. "Did you find everything you needed darling?", she asks.

"Yes ma'am, thank you.", I say.

"You're welcome darling.", she says as she waves to me as I go out the door.

I make it back to the cabin. I pull out my wand. I use a spell to gather branches for the fire pit. I get some string lights and use my wand to hang them on the trees that will be above us. I lay a few blankets and pillows on the ground. It looks beautiful.

I go inside and see Colin cooking. He is upgraded from basketball shorts to black sweatpants, still no shirt. I stop in the doorway and stare at him as he makes spaghetti. He has the table set with candles lit on the table.

I can feel myself blushing just by looking at him. His body is so defined and the way he clenches his jaw while he concentrates is too much for me.

"I went ahead and made lunch so we won't be in a rush for my surprise", Colin says.

"That is a great idea. It smells so good.", I say. He scoops a little bit of the sauce out of the pan. I open my mouth and he slides the spoon in. "Yum. I can't wait to eat. I'll start making the salad if you want me too?", I ask.

"Of course. I would love your help.", he answers.

Colin and I talk and clean as we cook together. After we get done eating I walk over to him, wrap my arms around his neck, and kiss him. "We have some time before your surprise. What do you want to do?", I say smiling.

I can see him thinking hard. His smile is the most beautiful thing I have ever seen. I love seeing him so happy. I miss the days when we were free of worry. But what is adventure without a mission, excitement, chaos, victory, or heartache?

"I want to play a board game. Do you remember when we would have game nights with your parents? You were always so competitive.", Colin says giggling.

"No I wasn't, I just do not like to lose." I say in a confident tone.

"Uh huh. Well then let's play twister. We won't be worried about winning, we'll be too busy laughing." Colin says.

I go into the kitchen and pull out twister. "I am going to switch into a tank top and shorts before we start." I say.

I come back downstairs after throwing on my clothes to Colin sitting on the floor with the game ready.

Colin jumps up and flicks the spinner at the sound of me reaching the bottom step. He lands on right hand on red. Before following through with his turn he looks up to see me. His jaw drops and then turns into a grin. "Distracting me again, I see?", Colin says.

"If anyone is distracting it is you.", I say as I look Colin up and down. I blush imagining touching his body. He rolls his eyes. I make my way to the spinner as he puts his right hand on red. I flick the spinner and I land on left foot on yellow.

Colin is already giggling. We can never be serious together when we play games. I think it makes it more fun. I finish my turn right as Colin lands on left hand on blue.

My mind freezes as he starts to do push ups. Every muscle in his back is showing. I get so flustered when I see him this way. I start to stutter, I can't stop smiling, and I get really clumsy. The sexier he is the more clutz I become.

I land on left hand on red. My hands are shaking and I am obviously sweating from the thoughts in my head. I bend slowly with my foot on yellow to put my hand on red.

Colins giggles have stopped. "Are you looking at my butt? I say taunting him as I peek through my legs.

Now he is blushing. "No never", he says flirting. He lands on left foot on green. He then throws his leg over me.

I am a giggling mess and I know any minute I am going to fall. Now it's my turn. I land on right hand on yellow. I am going to be a pretzel. I bend as much as I can and then reach my hand towards yellow. My pinky is so close. Between Colins laughter and my sweaty hands I am doomed. I feel his bare stomach and chest on me. My heart is pounding.

I finally get my pinky on yellow and then my leg slips out and down I go. I am laying on my back laughing and then I open my eyes. Colins beautiful blue eyes are staring back at me. I can barely think let alone come up with something to say.

His face slowly starts moving towards mine. I cannot contain myself when our lips meet. It is like fireworks as our mouths become one. His mouth claims mine with a fiery passion that sends heat all the way down to my stomach. He holds on to my waste so tight as if I am going to slip away.

I grasp his face with both hands deepening our kiss further. I pull back feeling the heat on my cheeks.

"Let's go up stairs and get ready and then we can go outside."he says grinning.

We both head upstairs. I throw on a wine red colored dress. It is short with ruffles at the bottom. I braid my hair back with a fall colored yellow ribbon.

Colin comes out of the bathroom in a navy blue button up, khaki pants, and his black hair is gelled back. He is concentrating on buttoning his top button. I hurry down the stairs.

His eyes lock on to mine when he gets to the top step. He takes him time walking down the stairs. His eyes never leave mine.

Colin's arms wrap around my waist in a swift movement the moment he leaves the last step. I feel like my smile is taking up all of my face. I can only imagine the shade of pink it is from me blushing.

I pull his head down to mine. My mouth meets his ear, "Close your eyes and no peeking", I whisper.

I take one of Colin's hands from my waist and lead him to the screen door and onto the porch. I place him to where he is facing the front yard right where I have the fire pit and everything set up.

"Open your eyes", I say.

Colin opens his eyes and smiles so big. WIthout saying a word he picks me up and carries me into the yard. He lays me down on the soft, thin, cream colored blanket. He lays next to me wrapping his arms around me. I can feel his muscles through his shirt. I feel so safe and warm. I gently move my fingertips down Colin's arm untill I reach the sleeve of his shirt. I look up at him and meet his gaze. He is looking into my eyes with so much happiness. I can feel the heat rising to my cheeks again. I quickly look down to hide that I am blushing. With a single finger Colin lifts up my head with my chin. In one motion he moves his finger from my chin to cupping my cheek with his hand. I lean my head into his hand. Melting into his touch. The wind blows causing me to shiver. Colin pulls me closer to him. There is no space between us now. Our faces are mere centimeters apart. I press my lips against his.

I feel like I could sit underneath the light of the moon and kiss him forever. We lay back together at the same time. Resting our heads on the pillows. I love the way the glow of the lights highlight his jawline, his blue eyes, and the way his lips curl up as he smiles down at me. Colin's smile lights up the world around me, more than the moon or string lights ever could.

I have always wondered what he was thinking when he looks at me this way. At first I would get nervous, but now it makes me feel beautiful. He runs his finger across my bottom lip then down to my chin. I shiver with anticipation, wanting him more and more. He pulls my face to his never breaking eye contact. His mouth claims mine. It is like time stops. I am lost in his touch, the smell of his cologne, and the taste of his mouth on mine. My whole body feels like it reacts to him. I can feel the heat rising in my stomach.

I get so lost in kissing him that I forget why we're outside. I stop kissing him just for a moment. "Do you want to do s'mores?"I ask, smiling.

Colin, still centimeters from my face whispers, "I don't know I am enjoying being this close to you."

"We can lay here and cuddle if you'd like. This is your surprise so I want to do whatever is going to make you happy."

"You always make me happy, love. Especially when I get to hold you like this.", Colin says, then he kisses my forehead.

"That sounds like heaven. You know? I could always just bring the s'mores to us?" I say. We sit up and I move on to Colins lap. I take out my wand, I make the chocolate and graham crackers float in the air, while I catch the marshmallows on fire. I quickly put them out and put everything together. Then the smores float to Colin and I.

He takes a big bite out of his, getting chocolate above his lip. I take my finger and wipe the chocolate away. Then I lick the chocolate off my finger. I take a bite of mine and I lick my fingers to get the chocolate off again.

I swallow my bite then look up to see that he is staring at me with nothing but huger in his eyes.

He grabs my face with both hands and starts kissing me slowly. I drop my s'more. I am all the way on his lap facing him. He takes one hand off of my face and moves his hand down my back. His hands are strong and warm. I love how gentle he is with me and how I can feel how much he loves me with every touch. He stops. I can see in his face that he is serious and that he is thinking hard about something.

"I love you, Amelia Jones. I don't know what the future holds, but I do know that I want everyday that I have on this earth to be with you. When Blaze took me away, I felt lost. There were moments that I felt like I couldn't breathe without you. Promise me that when Blaze comes back and we have to go to battle that you will be careful. I can't lose you. Losing my parents took a part of me that I have never gotten back. For a long time I wasn't truly happy. There was sadness around me all the time. But you've made that sadness go away over the years. You are my happiness. I can't live without you. I am so in love with you that I don't know what to do sometimes. I love everything about you. Your heart, your mind, your personality, your strength, your body, and every single thing else about you. My heart aches for you and my body yearns for yours. I am not whole until you are in my arms, until your hand is in mine, until I can taste your mouth on mine, until I can feel your heart racing as fast as mine, or until I can hear your beautiful voice and laugh. I am madly in love with you. All of you. I am yours. I have always been yours. I want to know only you, forever. And even then when I think about spending forever with you, it is still not enough time. My thoughts of you never end and neither does my deserie for you.", Colin says, looking deep into my eyes, searching for what I am thinking.

I put both of my hands on Colin's face, and say "I am not going anywhere. You are my future, my forever, and my soulmate. I can't promise that I won't get hurt. But I can promise that I am going to give that battle or any other fight we face everything that I have. I am yours just as much as you are mine. In your arms I am safe, my knees go weak when you kiss me, I can barely stand the heat that rises in my stomach when your fingers run through my hair, I can barely control myself when you kiss me, and my heart beats out of my chest when I am in your presence. My body yearns for yours just as much as yours does for me. I want you. I need you." I say then with all the passion building inside of me, I kiss him.

Colin picks me up and carries me into the cabin, never removing his mouth from mine. We come through the door so fast that it swings open. Our kiss is getting faster and hotter with every step we take. We make it up the stairs. Colin lays me down on the bed and stops. He looks deep into my eyes. "Is this too fast? We can stop?" Colin says, his eyes searching mine with concern in his voice.

"Colin, I want to. I want this. I love you. I want you, all of you.", I say, closing the space between us. I press my lips against his. I can feel the warmth of Colins tongue slide into my mouth slowly. He slides his hands down my hips and takes off my dress. Then he kisses my cheek, down my neck, to my chest, and back up to my lips.

My hands shake as I unbutton Colin's shirt, but I am not nervous. I grip the bottom of Colin's shirt and pull it over his head. I thought I would be nervous, but I am not. Colin slowly takes off the rest of my clothes. He gently runs his hand up and down my leg. His hands are trembling. His eyes never leave mine. They are searching for even the tiniest bit of doubt or nervousness. He then removes the rest of his clothes and climbs on top of me.

He kisses me softly, then stops. "Are you sure? I love you. We can wait if you want to. I want this to be perfect like you wanted it to be.", Colin says gently rubbing my face.

"Colin, I promise. You make it perfect.", I say, wrapping my arms around him. I kiss his lips, cheek, and then his neck. I hear him moan and grab onto the blanket.

The sound of his moan makes my heart beat even faster than it already was. "Stop holding back. I am ready. I want this Colin. I need you.", I say, looking into his eyes.

Colin kisses me deeper than he ever has before. He then places kisses all down my body until he starts pleasuring me. I grip the blankets so tight. I cannot help the moans and noises that escape me. He stops right as I cannot take any more. He then raises out from under the blanket. His hands rubbing all over my body. It's like he wants all of me. All at once. He gently caresses my face, "I am going to ease in. If it hurts, tell me to stop and I will. I nod my head yes, looking deep in his eyes. He slowly eases in. I feel the moisture on my thighs as I move my legs.

I moan out with nothing but pleasure as I feel him all the way inside me. Relief fills his eyes as sees that he is pleasuring me. I thought my first time would hurt, but I have never felt so good. Colin is being so easy and loving.

"I love you so much", Colin whispers into my ear as he goes in and out of me.

"I love you more" I say and then bite my lip. His whole body is still shaking.

It feels so good. Colin is breathing so heavy. I can feel his heart beating so fast on my chest. He starts moving faster and faster. It is like we are one. He grabs ahold of my waist and moves deeper in. I scream his name. I feel my legs shaking. I look into his eyes, losing myself with every motion and touch. I am in complete and utter bliss.

His moans bring me even more pleasure. I grab on to his neck and move up causing him to go even further in me. I scream out his name again. I can see him losing every ounce of control he has. It's enough to send me over the edge. We finish at the same time. Clenching onto each other's bodies as tight as we can. He gently places a kiss on my forehead. "That was perfect.", I whisper, still trying to catch my breath.

"Yes, yes it was love.", Colin whispers back to me. He slowly lays down next to me and pulls me into his arms. He pulls my hand to his lips. He kisses my finger tips. He then kisses my hand, all the way up my arm, my neck, and then my lips.

"You are not in any pain are you?"Colin whispers, gently rubbing my face.

"I am a little sore, but I have never felt better. That was more than I could have ever imagined. I love you so much", I say, nuzzling my head into his chest.

"It was, wasn't it. I love you more, Amelia Jones.", Colin says, beaming with happiness.

We did it. We really made love for the first time. I have read about what it feels like many times in romance novels. None of it came close to describing how Colin made me feel though. I could make love to him over and over again.

Chapter Four

Colin

I wake up to Amelia still laying on my chest. She looks so beautiful. I gently brush the hair out of her face. Her eyes crack open a little bit and she smiles. " Good morning", she says.

I pull her face to mine and kiss her. " Good morning, how are you feeling?", I ask.

"I feel good. I am just still a little tired. I am going to go take a shower. Do you want to shower with me and then we can make breakfast together?"

"Sounds perfect," I say."

Amelia sits up and pulls the sheet around her as she stands up out of the bed. I am in shock at the sight of blood on it. I immediately jump out of bed. I pick her up and carry her into the bathroom.

"I am so sorry. Are you okay? I didn't mean to hurt you.", I say with panic in my voice.

"Colin, it's okay. This is normal. I am a little sore, but I'll be okay. Please don't feel bad. Last night was so wonderful and you were perfect.", she says smiling.

"I love you more. I would never forgive myself if I hurt you. Especially if I hurt you while making love to you." I say as I turn the water on.

I help Amelia into the bath tub. I pour soap in and watch the bubbles grow around her. I get in behind her. I pour soap onto her sponge and wash her back for her. I move her hair to the side and I kiss her neck then I rest my head on her shoulder As she washes the rest of her body I wrap my arms around her.

I shouldn't have freakout the way I did. But I just felt so much guilt all at once when I looked at the sheet. But she is right. Last night was perfect. I would not have it any other way.

Once we get out of the shower I change the sheets. Amelia lays on the bed in her towel. I prop her feet up, lay a blanket on her, and kiss her forehead gently.

"Stop worrying. I am okay." Amelia says, smiling, pulling me in for another kiss.

"I will stop worrying when you have some food in your belly. What do you want for breakfast? I will even serve it to you in bed. So you can just lay here and rest." I say brushing my hand against her face.

"You are adorable. How did I ever get so lucky? I want some waffles and bacon pretty please.", Amelia says as she bats her eyes at me.

"You got it.", I say as I go downstairs and into the kitchen.

I make Amelia and I breakfast. I add strawberries and whipped cream to her waffles and blueberries to mine. I get the breakfast tray out of the cabinet, I add our plates, and our glasses of orange juices to the tray. Once I get upstairs I sit our food on the nightstand before looking at Amelia. I look up to see that she is painting her fingernails. The sun is coming in from the window, her hair is pulled up in a messy bun, and she is wearing one of my tshirts.

I stand here, not moving, for just a moment, admiring her. "You look so beautiful", I say to her smiling.

"Thank you. The food smells amazing." she says quietly. I can sense a small amount of sadness in her voice.

"Is everything okay love?" I ask worriedly.

"Yes, everything is okay. I was just thinking about your mom.

Every time I paint my nails, I braid my hair, or I wear the pearls that she gave me for my tenth birthday, I feel like she is here with me."

I crawl onto the bed and put my arm around her. "The day you went to camp she said she was going to have a girls day with my mom and I the next day. But we didnt get to. Some of my favorite memories as a little girl are my mother, Kate, and I dressing up in pretty dresses, wearing pearls, and high heels. Your mom would do my makeup while my mother cleared the furniture out of the way in the living room. We would turn on music, laugh, and dance together. Just us girls. I would give anything to be able to have a girls day with her one more time. I miss her so much." she says looking off into the distance.

"I miss her too. Every single day. Honestly more like every second that I breathe. I miss her being the first person that I talked to when I would come downstairs for breakfast, I miss her voice, hearing her laugh, and how she always smelled so good. She always knew what to say and do. She would be so proud of you, Amelia." I say then I brush the hair out of her face.

"I hope so. I know Joseph and Kate are very proud of the man you have grown up to be. I know you miss them even more than I do. I am sorry for bringing this up. You have made breakfast and everything. I shouldn't have mentioned it.", Amelia says, putting her head down.

"Do not say that. I love talking about my mother and father. Especially memories as special as the ones that you shared with her. I always want you to be honest with me about how you feel. You have always been honest with me. I have never questioned telling you something or letting you in. Just because we are adults now and we made love last night does not mean our relationship needs to change. If anything, our trust should grow. I never ever want you to feel like you have to hide your feelings to spare my own. Especially if it is about my mother and father. I was not the only one that lost them, love. You lost them too. You do not have to be strong for me. I want to always be the person you go to whether you are feeling happy, sad, strong, weak, angry, or any other emotion. Please don't feel bad. We are still having an amazing morning.", I say then I grab the breakfast tray off of the night stand and place it on the bed in front of Amelia and I.

"You are my safe place. I know in my heart that I can tell you anything. But I also want to make you happy. I just never want to be the person that takes your smile away. I promise I will always tell you how I feel no matter what. I trust you. I always have. After last night I feel closer to you than I ever thought was possible. I know I do not have to be strong for you. I think your parents would be proud of our love. I am so thankful that you learned how to love from them. One day when we have a baby of our own we can tell them all about their amazing grandparents and all their adventures. They will know that their daddy is the man he is because he was so loved.", she says then she gently strokes my face with her hand.

"Watching you be a mother is going to be the best part about us becoming parents. I just know you are going to be perfect. You will be gentle like Grace and protective like Seth. They have raised an exceptional daughter. I am going to be the luckiest man in the world to get to marry you and spend the rest of my life with you. Even though my parents will not be able to physically be a part of our lives. I know that their spirits will always be watching over us. We will always love them and remember them. Just like our children will. Our food is getting cold though, so we need to eat.", I say jokingly.

She looks at the food excitedly, ``It looks so good. You really are the best, you know that?.", she says, winking at me. I cut a piece of her waffle and put a bite into her mouth. She licks her lips and smiles. Before she can say a word I place my lips on hers.

"I love you so much." I say pulling back and smiling at her.

"I love you more.", She says, smiling back at me.

We finish our food and walk downstairs together. I sit down on the couch and pull her onto my lap. We spend the rest of the morning cuddled up on the couch while I read to her.

We must've fallen asleep because I wake up to Shadow right in front of my face meowing at me. Amelia is still asleep. It is still light outside. I scoot out from under her so I can get off the couch.

Someone is here. I can feel it. I walk to the screen door. I am shocked to see Blaze sitting on the porch swing. I swing open the screen door. He stands up and I immediately hug him.

My hug catches him off guard. He makes a grunting sound but then I feel him smile and his arms wrap around me. I have missed him so much.

"Is everything okay?", I ask quickly. Realizing that there must be something wrong if he is here.

"Unfortunately no. I was back in Ohio with some witches that I have gathered when I got an urgent letter from Amelia's father. Her grandmother left. It was two days ago. She left a note saying that she had to leave and that she will meet us in Ohio where the serpents are at, in exactly five days. We're already on day three so we are going to have to hurry. Before coming here I had to take the witches that agreed to help me to Amelia's father. They'll be staying in your old house with Jack, Amber, and Ace. Three of them are prior members of the serpents, two of them are witches that are old friends of your father, and then the last one is Amber's little brother. I'll give you details about them later, but right now you have to go get Amelia. We have to leave as soon as possible.", Blaze says

"Amelia is going to be worried sick about her grandmother," I say.

"Amelia's grandmother is strong. She is going to be okay. She knows what she is doing. We have to trust her.", Blaze says confidently.

"You're right. I just wish someone knew what she was doing so we could help.", I say.

"I think that's why she left. It is something she has to do alone. I understand. I have been in situations where I had to do things alone. Sometimes the best way you can help is not helping at all. Until that person is ready.", Blaze says.

Blaze picks up shadow and walks inside. I follow behind him. The sound of the door opening wakes Amelia. She sits up. Her eyes open wide when she sees Blaze. She smiles really big but then the smile quickly fades.

Blaze explains everything to Amelia like how he did to me. She starts to cry. I sit down on the couch and hold her. "She will be okay.", I say, wiping the tears from her face.

"I am sorry that I had to bring such bad news, but we really do have to hurry. The faster we make it back the faster we can get to where the serpents are.", Blaze says as he sits down at the kitchen table.

I help Amelia up and we walk upstairs together. "I am so sorry all this is happening.", I say with my head down as I put clothes in a bag. Amelia walks over to me, gently places her hand on my cheek, makes eye contact with me, and says "None of this is your fault. The serpents are the ones to blame. My grandmother has a plan. I can feel it. We are going to make sure that they can never hurt anyone else ever again."

She kisses me and then begins to pack her bag. We come downstairs to Blaze still sitting at the table. "Are you hungry? We can make something before we leave if you want", I say to him.

"No, it's fine. We can have dinner with Amelia's family once we get back. Jack, Amber, and Ace have been enjoying Grace's cooking. Seth and Ace have become quite close from what I could tell yesterday. Before we leave I want to tell you both about the witches I have gathered. Amber's little brother's name is Troy. He is a lot like Amber. You have to earn his trust. He is eighteen like you guys, so he is still learning. But don't underestimate him. He is very strong. The three witches that are prior serpents are Luke, Alice, and Oliver. They are also eighteen. They were recruited by the serpents when they were only thirteen. They have been through a lot. When they were sixteen they decided that they were done with the serpents and broke out. Since then they have tried three different times to break out others, but each time they had to flee. Then there are Joseph's old friends. Reid and Martin. I am going to warn you both now, they don't like me. Do not get offended if they are rude or arrogant towards me. It does not bother me, so it should not bother either of you. We need their help, so I will put up with them for the sake of defeating Ethan and all of his followers.

"I won't let anyone mistreat you. I don't care how powerful they think they are. My father would not want them to be mean to you.", I say, trying to stay calm.

"Now now, nephew. There is no reason to get emotional on me. I was a different person when your father was friends with them. We were all young and I was angry. Joseph tried to help me in his own way. I just didn't want his help. His friends didn't like me then and they probably never will. I did and said a lot of things I can't take back.", Blaze says in his serious voice.

"But that's not who you are now? They should give you a chance. Obviously you are trying now. Why can't they just give you a break?" Amelia says in an angry voice.

Blaze and I both look at Amelia in shock. She hadn't said a word or made a sound this whole time.

I giggle under my breath, thinking about how she is just as protective as her parents.

"While I appreciate the fact that you both care. I must remind you guys that I really do not care what they think. Now, I am going to go outside with Shadow and get on my broom. I will give you both a moment and then you can meet me outside." Blaze says then walks out the door.

"I don't like those guys already', Amelia says, rolling her eyes.

"I don't either. But like Blaze said we really do need their help. So we can just deal with them until after we defeat the serpents. Then we won't have to see them again. Everything is going to be okay. Please come here?"I gesture for Amelia to come to me.

Amelia walks over to me and wraps her arms around my neck. "I love you.", I say as I stroke her face. She smiles up at me with the most radiant smile I have ever seen. You would think after all these years of looking into her eyes and seeing her beautiful smile that I wouldn't be as captivated by her as I am. But all the years do is make me fall more and more in love with her. I could look into her eyes and kiss her lips for the rest of my life and still be madly in love with her every time.

"I love you too, Colin.", she says. Amelia leans her face into my hand as I stroke her face. I love hearing her say my name. I always have. I can't help the smile taking over my face.

"What is it?"Amelia says, giggling.

"Nothing. I am just crazy about you, that's all.", I say.

"You amaze me with the way that you always know just what to say."Amelia says, smiling ear to ear.

WIthout responding I place my lips on hers. I pull her in close and savor the feeling of her lips on mine, her body up against me, the feeling of her hair in between my fingers, and the sweet smell of her vanilla scented perfume.

I reluctantly let go, "We have to go", I say. I wrap my hand in hers as we walk outside together.

Blaze has our broom ready next to his. Shadow is sitting on his shoulder. Amelia and I get on our broom together.

"I am so excited to see everyone," Amelia says, with an overwhelming amount of excitement in her voice.

"Everyone is definitely ready to see you both. Now let's go", Blaze says as he takes off into the sky.

I turn around, kiss Amelia, and take off into the sky behind Blaze.

I do not know what future awaits us or if we will make it out of this battle alive. But what I do know is that I could not choose better people to fight alongside me.

Chapter Five

Amelia

I can see my mother standing outside our house when we arrive. She looks so beautiful.

Her brown curls sway in the wind. Between the tears and the moonlight her eyes sparkle. I immediately jump off of mine and Colin's broom and run to her.

Tears start rolling down my face before I can even reach her. I almost knock her over as she pulls me in for a hug. I hold on to her as tight as I can, with fear that if I let go, she might just be a dream.

Still grasping her arms I look up to see my father is now standing in the doorway. He has tears in his eyes and his cheeks are bright red. He practically leaps to my mother and I. He picks me up and spins me around like he did when I was a little girl.

I fly through the air taking in every second. Every moment that I ever took for granted I regret. Seeing them everyday, hearing their voices, laughing with them, and knowing that I could just hug them anytime.

From now on I will cherish every word they speak and every breath they take.

You would think Colin's parents passing away would have made me think this way. But it was like in my mind nothing could happen to them. They were all Colin and I had so not having them every moment was not an option.

"Oh honey, we have missed you so much. Both of you", my mother says as she reaches out to Colin. My father pulls us all in for a group hug. When he lets go we go inside. My mother already has the table set and the food is ready. My mother made a big pot of chicken and dumplings, mashed potatoes, gravy, and rolls. It smells so good.

Colin puts his arm around my hip as we walk in together. I smile down at his hand. We walk into the kitchen and I see Stella standing in front of the kitchen table waiting on us. Colin moves his hand and I run to Stella wrapping my arms around her. We start jumping up and down together yelling as loud as we can with happiness. "I've missed you so much!!" I yell.

"I've missed you so much more. After dinner we are going upstairs for girl talk. I need all the details." Stella says winking at Colin and I. I swat at her laughing.

Colin and I sit next to each other. Stella sits across from me. My mother sits next to my father and my grandfather. My grandfather's eyes are so sad. He isn't eating. All he has in front of him is a glass of water. I get up, go around the table, and give him a hug. "I am so sorry about grandma. We are going to get her back. No matter what.", I say.

My grandfather pats me and says "I know dear. I just miss her a lot. When you are with someone for as long as your grandmother and I have been together, it feels empty without them. She has always been stubborn and strong. It's one of the reasons I fell in love with her. Your grandma says she sees a lot of herself in you. I am proud of your grandmother, just like I am proud of you."

"I love that I am like her. I can only hope that I am as strong and fearless as her one day.", I say.

I hug my grandfather one more time before going back to my seat. Before we start eating Jack, Ace, Blaze, Amber, and Troy come in. Following behind them is Luke, Alice, Oliver, Martin, and Reid.

Troy is Tall, but really muscular at the same time, he has dirty blonde hair, freckles, and golden brown eyes. Luke looks like he is a little bit shorter than Colin. He has red hair, green eyes, and pale skin. Alice is biracial. She has long curly hair, bright green eyes, and a beautiful smile. Oliver is black. He is also really tall and muscular. He has kind eyes that are a grayish blue color.

Martin is a little bit smaller than my father. He has brown hair, brown eyes, and a serious face. Reid is about the same size as Martin. He also has brown hair but he has blue eyes.

I see him look at Colin as he walks in. Colin makes eye contact with him. I squeeze Colin's hand. He looks away from Reid, brings my hand to his lips, kisses it, and then smiles at me.

I have always loved the way that Colin silently reassures me that he is okay.

Blaze comes and sits next to Colin. My father pulls out his wand and does a spell to make the table longer and more chairs appear. Everyone else takes a seat.

Everyone catches up and talks while they eat. Oliver sits next to Stella. I can tell that she thinks he's cute. She keeps playing with her hair as she talks. Hannah is talking to Troy. They seem to be getting along well, but I can tell that he is quiet. Martin and Reid are talking to each other. Every now and then Reid looks at Colin and looks away.

"You look just like your father", Reid says to Colin.

Everyone stops eating and looks at Colin except Blaze. Blaze is looking down at his plate. "Thank you.", Colin says, making eye contact with Reid.

I can feel Colin's hand tense up.

"Your father was a good man. He would be proud of you. I know we are. Seth and Grace you have taken such good care of him. Thank you." Reid says.

Before my parents or Colin can say anything I quickly say, "Blaze has also done a great job of taking care of Colin."

Reid looks at me and then shoots a glare at Blaze.

"I am done eating. Are you done eating Amelia?"Stella says,

trying to stop any conflict that is about to happen.

"Yes I am done eating." I say calmly to Stella. I kiss Colin and excuse myself from the table. Stella grabs my hand and quickly runs us up the stairs.

We walk into my bedroom and I sit on my bed. Stella shuts the door and says, "what was that about?! You totally don't like that Reid guy."

"It's not that I don't like him. I am just not going to let him disrespect Blaze. Especially in my house. Blaze loves colin. He is trying his best. Reid was Collin's father's friend when they were young. I get that Blaze wasn't the best in the past. But that doesn't mean that Reid gets to be mean to him now.", I say.

"I understand that. All we can do is love Blaze. Things just need to be peaceful in the house. We all have to get along and work together. Enough about that Reid guy though. How was your time with Colin?! Tell me everything!" Stella says smiling ear to ear.

"It was amazing. We spent so much time together talking, training, and well uhh other things.", I say giggling.

"Noooooo. You didn't?! You did?! How was it?", says Stella, jumping on the bed excitedly.

"It was perfect. When I woke up I thought it was a dream. Colin was so sweet and loving the whole time. Making love to him was even better than I imagined. He was so tender, slow, and romantic. He even helped me bathe the next morning.".I say smiling as I think about Colin.

"That is so sweet. You guys are perfect together. I cannot believe he helped you bathe. That is so romantic.", Stella says.

"So you and Oliver?!", I say laughing.

"What are you talking about?!" Stella says blushing.

"You know exactly what I am talking about. I saw you staring at him and flirting." I say, winking at her.

I have missed Stella so much. I don't know what I would have done if I would have lost her that day of the battle. She is my best friend. I love how happy she is all the time. No matter how I am feeling or what I go through she comes in with a positive attitude and makes it all better.

Stella rolls her eyes. Then we lay back on the bed as she catches me up on everythings that's happened since I've been gone.

"I have a surprise for you. We have to go over to the mirror. Then you have to close your eyes.", Stella says. We walk over to the mirror. I am so curious and excited.

I close my eyes. I hear Stella whispering a spell.

"Now open your eyes. I made this spell for you so that way anytime we are apart you can still have beautiful makeup. I wrote it down for you and put it in your vanity draw. I know you love the way I do it. So now it'll be like I did your makeup for you even when I didn't physically do it.", Stella says, smiling, twirling her wand." I look into the mirror. My makeup is perfect. My eyeshadow is a rust orange color, my lipstick is burgundy, my eyeliner is perfect, and my blush is plum. "I love it! Thank you! I can't believe you thought of doing this for me. You are the best.", I say to stella.

"Oh it's nothing. I just really missed doing your makeup while you were gone. It was really lonely without you here. I am so glad that you are back.", Stella says in a sweet voice.

"Me too. I missed you so much. There was so many times that I wanted to talk to you, see you, and hug you." I say as I get into my closet. I pick out a wine colored dress and my jean jacket. I grab my shoes and put them on.

"I missed you too. I am just so glad that we can have all the girl talk we want now. I'll do your hair!"Stella, sits me down at my vanity. She brushes my hair, braids two strands, and then pins them back on each side. She then curls the ends of my hair.

"Colin won't be able to keep his eye off of you tonight. We should all do something together later." Stella says excitedly.

"That is a great idea! We should all go out to the treehouse and have a sleepover." I say.

"Perfect", Stella says, leaping towards the door.

Chapter Six
Colin

I watch Amelia go upstairs with Stella. I turn to look at Seth and ask, "Can you come talk to me outside for a moment?" and then I turn to Blaze and ask, "Will you come join us as well?"

Blaze looks up from his plate with confusion on his face. Seth kisses Grace and follows Blaze and I out the door.

"I asked you guys out here because you both mean a lot to me. Seth, you have been like a father to me since I was born. From as far back as I remember you have loved me and treated me like family. I know that I would not be who I am today without you. I will never be able to repay you and Grace for everything you have done for me. I love you both so much.

Blaze, you didn't have to come get me. But you did. You have taught me so much. You are so much more than my uncle. I can't imagine my life without you now. I trust you with my life. I love you and no matter what anyone thinks, just know I am proud of you.

With that being said, I need to ask you both something. Seth, I want to ask your permission to marry Amelia. I know we're about to go to battle and everything, but life is unexpected and you never know what is going to happen.

Blaze, I want to ask you to be my best man. I mean it when I say that you are more than my uncle. You are my best friend.", I say, trying not to sound nervous.

"Colin, you have always felt like a son to me. So having you as a son in law will just be adding a title to an already wonderful relationship. I have loved you your whole life. I couldn't pick a better man for my daughter. Of course you have my blessing. Grace and I will be honored to watch you all get married. I only wish that your parents could be here to see it as well. They would be so proud of the man that you have grown up to be. I know I am." Seth says with tears in his eyes. He pulls me in for a hug. He lets go and dries his tears.

"Thank you. You have no idea how much that means to me." I say as my voice cracks.

Blaze has his head down. When he raises his head his eyes are red and full of tears. "I would love to be your best man. I don't deserve it, but I am truly honored. I wish your father and I would have had a better relationship. Maybe then I could have been in your life sooner than what I was. I love you nephew. Thank you for what you said. You have given me a second chance at life. I won't let you down like how I let Joseph down. I promise." Blaze says, putting his head back down.

I walk over to him and hug him tight. "Keep your head held high.", I whisper in his ear as I let go.

"I am going to propose tonight. I know we're all supposed to leave out first thing in the morning so I don't have a lot of time. I am going to go up in the treehouse and wait for her and then I am going to propose with my mothers wedding ring. I know it would mean a lot to my mother and father. What I need you guys to do is get Amelia to go into the treehouse without her expecting anything. So that way it is a surprise. Then once she comes up everyone can hurry to the bottom of the treehouse and listen. Amelia loves pictures, so if you guys could tell Stella to sneak up the ladder somehow and take pictures that would be great. Oh and will you get Jack to bring me a button up shirt?", I say laughing.

"You got it. Blaze and I will handle everything. All you need to do is go get in the treehouse."Seth says confidently.

Blaze looks at Seth with a worried look and then back at me. "Yeah we've got this", Blaze says with a not so confident voice.

I laugh to myself as I walk away. I climb up into the treehouse. I pull out my wand to decorate the tree house. I clean everything up, relight the string lights, and I put flower petals on the floor of the treehouse. I can feel my heart beating out of my chest. I don't know why I am so nervous. Amelia and I have already talked about getting married, so I know she is going to say yes. I just want to make sure this moment is perfect.

"Here" Jack whispers as he throws the shirt up into the treehouse.

"Thank you", I whisper back.

"Why do you sound so nervous? You and Amelia were made for each other. Amelia's dad is going to have her mom help Stella with the surprise. I'm surprised Amelia didn't hear her mom screaming when her dad told her. Blaze is quietly rounding everyone up and telling them what is going on. We're going to have Stella ask Amelia to go to the treehouse with her. Stella will come up with something. Then once they go out the backdoor the rest of us will go out the front door, around the house, and hide where Amelia can't see us. Then once you pop the question, and she says yes of course, we're all going to set off fireworks with our wands for you guys. That was her mom's idea. Just breathe. You're going to do great. What's the worst that could happen? You get nervous and fall out of the treehouse?" Jack says laughing as he walks away.

"Not funny!" I yell at him.

Amelia is going to be so happy. I can't wait to see her beautiful smile and hear her say yes. I will remember this day for the rest of my life. This treehouse means a lot to Amelia and I. It is full of so many good memories, adventures, and beautiful nights falling asleep under the stars. It also has bad memories. I know how hard it was for her to come up here after my parents were killed. But I think that also has beauty in it. Life is always going to have good and bad. It's the balance of life. We just have to always remember the good, so that way the bad doesn't seem as big. We made a million amazing memories in our treehouse before that awful night. It was "our place". I can't think of a better place to ask Amelia to spend the rest of her life with me. For better or for worse. We can get through anything together.

She is my happiness, my light, and my best friend.

Chapter Seven

Amelia

There is a knock on my door right as Stella is about to open it. "Come in", I say.

"It's just me dear. Your mother wants Stella to come down stairs and help her with something.", my father says.

Stella looks at my father with a confused look and then at me. Then walks out the door.

"Does mom need my help too?" I ask.

"No. It was just something small I think. Your mother and I are so happy that you are home. Your Grandmother is going to be so proud of you when she sees you. You have grown up to be such a strong and beautiful young woman. Tomorrow is going to be hard. Promise me that tonight you will let yourself have fun, please? Your grandmother is the strongest person I have ever met. I know in my heart that she is okay. No one can hurt her.", My father says, pulling me in for a hug.

"I love you. I just want to get to her as soon as possible. I just need to see her and see that she is okay. Then we can bring her home. But I do promise to enjoy myself tonight. I have missed everyone so much. I'm excited to get to talk to everyone.", I say.

The door opens, "sorry to interrupt, Grace is asking for you guys.", Blaze says.

My father and I walk down stairs together with Blaze. My mother and Stella are in the kitchen cooking. "Honey you look so beautiful, Stella and I are finishing up. I wanted to ask you what sounds good for dessert?", my mother asks, she is smiling really big.

"Brownies sound good.", I say, smiling back at my mom.

"Okay darling. I've got this. You girls can go ahead and finish what you were doing now.", my mother says excitedly.

"Let's go to the treehouse. Blaze, will you go get Colin and tell him to meet us out there?" Stella says to Blaze.

Stella smiles back at my mom, loops her arm around mine, and leads me out the back door.

"It is such a beautiful night", I say to stella.

"It's perfect", Stella says, in a high pitched happy tone.

"Perfect for what?" I ask.

"Our sleepover of course. Go on up, I have to grab some more snacks.", she bends down and gets into a bag that is under the treehouse. I go ahead and climb up,"Stella says quickly.

I reach the top. I am speechless as I look around. Colin is in front of me on one knee.

The tree house is so beautiful.

"Amelia Skye Jones, you have been my best friend since I took my first breath. The world knew I was going to need someone by my side to get me through life. That person is you. I was so lost when my parents died, but you and your parents never let me forget how much you guys loved me. I always wanted a love like my parents had. I know without a doubt that you and I have that kind of love. You mean everything to me. I want to fall asleep reading to you and playing with your hair for the rest of my life. I want to lay under the stars with our children one day and tell them stories about us. I want to spend every moment that I have on this earth loving you and being the man you deserve. With magic or my bare hands, I will do whatever it takes to keep you safe and take care of you. I promise to love you now and for the rest of my days. Will you please do me the honor of becoming my wife?" Colin says.

"Yes of course, yes!!"I scream, as I ruin my makeup with all the tears.

He slides the ring on my finger. It fits perfectly. Then he picks me up off the ground, spins me around, and kisses me. It is a beautiful gold band, with a small diamond in the middle, and there is something engraved on the ring. "Our magical love". It is perfect.

"It was my mothers", Colin says, rubbing my finger.

"Oh Colin. It's beautiful. I love you so much. I can't wait to marry you.", I say crying.

Colin wipes away my tears and kisses me again.

"You guys are so perfect.", Stella says crying. Her makeup is just as messed up as mine.

I turn around and see Stella standing on the ladder with her camera. I start laughing hysterically and lift her up into the treehouse. When I bend down to pull her up I see my mother and father crying and everyone else standing around them. Blaze is trying to wipe away his tears before we see them.

"You guys knew? This is all so perfect. I love all of you so much.", I say crying and laughing at the same time.

"Wait let me fix your face", Stella says with a flick of her wand. I giggle and point to her face. She flicks her wand again and all her streak marks disappear.After squeezing Stella Colin helps me down the ladder.

As we climb down everyone starts lighting off fireworks. It is like a dream.

I run to my parents and they pull me into their arms. "I am so happy for you sweetheart. We know Colin loves you just as much as we do.", my mother says.

"I appreciate that he asked me for my blessing, but honestly he has had it for a long time. Colin is the type of man that fathers pray that their daughters marry.", my father says, shaking Colin's hand and then he pulls him in for a hug. I see Blaze walk inside. Everyone else comes up to me to look at the ring and congratulate us.

"Can I blow stuff up at your wedding?" Wesley asks. His mom hushes him.

"Umm, maybe not at the wedding. But, you can blow up as much stuff as you want at the battle?" I say laughing.

"Deal!"Wesley says excitedly.

"You look gorgeous. I've missed you.", Leah says.

"Thank you! I have missed you too!" I have a few spells that I need to work on with you and Stella before we leave tomorrow.

"Sounds good we can all meet outside first thing in the morning.", Leah says. Stella shakes her head in agreement.

"I need to get my camera inside. I want to get these pictures printed off. I'll hang them on your picture wall for you.", Stella says excitedly.

"Oh that sounds great! We can all go inside and eat brownies. Can Colin and I have a moment out here alone though, before we go inside, please?" I ask, smiling at everyone.

"Of course, honey.", my mother says as she ushers everyone inside.

"Wait, I want a picture with the photographer first.", I say to Stella.

Colin grabs the camera from Stella.

Stella and I wrap our arms around each other so tight. Our happiness pours from our smiles as we cheese for the camera.

She takes the camera from Colin. She turns around right as she reaches the backdoor, "I cannot wait to be a part of the beautiful life that you guys are going to share.", she says with the happiest voice I have ever heard.

I lean my head on Colin's chest. He wraps his arms around me. The night air is cool. It is so quiet and peaceful. I can hear the sound of Colin's heart beat. A few minutes go by. He raises my head up to look into my eyes. "I can't believe you are going to be my wife. I know we have talked about it, but it's different now that is actually going to happen. I love you so much. My Amelia Skye White. It sounds good, doesn't it?"Colin says grinning.

"It sounds perfect. I can't believe you did all this for me. But then again I can. You have always made me feel so special. Tonight was like a dream come true. I am so glad that my family got to be a part of it. I just wish my grandmother was here too. I can't wait to see her and talk to her.", I say.

"I know, love. We're going to get to her as fast as we can. Everything is going to be okay. I promise. Now there is one more thing I want us to do before we go inside.", Colin says, taking my hand in his.

"What might that be?" I ask Colin.

"May I have this dance?", Colin asks

"I would love to.", I say, batting my eyelashes.

Colin smiles and twirls me around and around. It feels effortless. He dips me as I come back around. I have my arms wrapped around his neck. I let go. His arms are tight around me. I can feel his muscles through his shirt. As I raise back up to meet his gaze, his blue eyes shine in the dark. He caresses my face as his lips meet mine. Then he twirls me around again. I put both my hands on his face and kiss him deeply, slowly, and passionately. The world around us starts to fade. It is just us, holding each other, swaying back and forth in the moonlight.

Chapter Eight
Colin

I walk inside and sit down at the kitchen table with Amelia. Her mother brings us brownies. Blaze, Stella, and Oliver sit in front of us. Amber sits next to me. Her brother decides to go back outside and train some more before he goes to bed. Leah and Hannah join him.

Ace sits next to Amelia's father. Martin and Reid stand next to the kitchen table talking back and forth. Reid glances at Blaze and I every now and then. It is really starting to get to me, but I am not going to cause a scene in Amelia's house.

"I would love for you to be my maid of honor, Stella", Amelia says to Stella.

"Of course! I would love to. I cannot wait to do your hair and makeup. Oh we have to go wedding dress shopping with your mom asap. You are going to look beautiful.", Stella says, whipping her notebook out to draw up some ideas.

"I agree. She is going to be the most beautiful bride.", I say to Amelia, kissing her on the cheek. She smiles at me. I wrap my arms around her and pull her in close. I love the feeling of her head resting on my shoulder.

"Who is going to be your best man?"Reid asks.

Seth and Ace stop their conversation; they both look at Blaze.

Amelia sits up and makes eye contact with Reid. I know she is getting ready to get protective if Reid says anything out of the way. Blaze has his head down, but I know he is listening.

"I asked Blaze to be my best man earlier when I asked Seth for his blessing to propose to Amelia. He said yes, so he is going to be my best man.", I say calmly and politely, trying to not instigate conflict.

Reid makes a face in Blaze's direction, but he keeps his head down.

"Do you think your father would want that? Joseph didn't even invite him to his own wedding. Has he ever told you how he got the scar under his eye? He didn't want bad people following Blaze and it affecting you and your mother. Look what it is doing to your life. You were fine until he came into your life. You had to go into hiding not once but twice. It's even affecting your girl and her family. The worst part is, he was in the group that killed your parents," Reid says anger and disgust in his voice.

"Now that is enough.", Seth says. As he stands up from the table.

The room is silent. I can feel the sweat on my forehead. Amelia looks like she could scream. Blaze has not moved an inch. Grace has tears in her eyes. Ace's face is so red. Jack is livid. He looks like he could attack Reid at any moment.

Reid has no right to talk about what my parents would want or their decisions. I don't even know him.

I let go of Amelia as I stand up from the table. I nod to Seth to let him know that I have the situation handled. He nods back and then sits down. He puts his arms around Grace. Amber puts her hand on her robe pocket where her wand is.

I have to watch my words carefully. I do not want this to turn into a fight between everyone.

"You might have known a version of Blaze at one time. But you do not know the man that he is today. It is unfortunate that you are not giving him the chance to show you. He is honest, protective, strong, and selfless. My parents were killed because they were good people. They killed an evil man that just so happened to be Ethan's son. Blaze was already in the group when it happened. I don't blame my father for not having that version of Blaze in our life. But what I do know is that he would be so proud of him if he were here today. Blaze is the only good thing that came from my parents passing. He didn't have to come here to take care of me when my parents passed, but he did. He is an amazing uncle, teacher, and friend. I am lucky to have him. Honestly we are all lucky to have him. Everything that is happening right now with the serpents is on them, not Blaze. Plus, I don't mean to be rude or anything, but my father didn't have you in his life either. I have never met you until now. I am glad that you are willing to be here and that you are willing to help. But if you cannot be civil and respectful to Blaze, then I will have to ask you to leave.", I say, in a calm, but serious tone.

Blaze looks up at me. His eyes are sad. It is the first time that he has lifted his head to acknowledge the conversation. He gets up and walks out the front door. I hurry to follow him outside. I can hear Reid saying something to me as I go out the door, but I don't stop.

Blaze stops at the front door of my old house. He turns around to face me. "Thank you for taking up for me in there. There is a part of me that feels like I do not deserve it though. I wasn't there for Joseph the way I should have been. I never listened to him. He knew dark magic was not worth the risk. When our parents died he got really angry. Dark magic had taken our parents away from us when he was eighteen and I was sixteen. You already know that I was a part of the serpents at the point, but back then that's when Joseph found out. He was furious. It wasn't a serpent that killed our parents. Your father didn't care though. He just cared that I could be a part of a group with dark witches in the first place. It kills me that his fate was sealed by a serpent. If I would have known that the serpents would be the cause of my brother's death back then I would have gotten out when he told me too. But instead I was foolish. We fought. We were both full of grief, rage, and pride. Neither one of us was willing to budge on our beliefs. During our fight Joseph gave me this scar. I could tell the moment he said the spell he regretted it. But it was too late. It had already hit me in the face. I didn't speak or see him again until I found out your mother was pregnant. I didn't come around because I wanted to respect your fathers wishes. My biggest regret is not making it to your house on time that night to save them. I should have been there.", Blaze says with a low voice.

I can see the pain in his eyes. "You can't change the past. You can only decide who you are going to be from now on. From the first day you came into Amelia's house until now you have been the uncle that my father would have wanted you to be. That is all that matters.", I say. I take a step and pull Blaze in for a hug.

"I love you, Colin, I think I am going to call it a night. I will be up when the sun comes up to get everyone ready."Blaze says, hugging me back and then he pulls away.

"Okay, sounds good." I say, in an unsure voice.

"I'm okay. Really. It'll take more than Reids judgment to get me down. I just wanted to make sure you knew that I loved your father and I regret not being there. I promise to always be there for you now though. For as long as I live.", Blaze says, opening the door.

"I love you. I know you will. Goodnight.", I say.

Blaze says, "I love you too. Goodnight", then closes the door behind him.

I walk back over to Amelia's house. Amber is sitting on the porch outside the door.

"Are you okay", I ask.

"Yeah. I just needed some air. Is Blaze okay?"she asks in a worried tone.

"He is okay. I think he just needed me to know his side of the story. He said something about going to bed, but if you hurry you might be able to catch him before he goes to sleep." I say.

"Oh no, it's okay. He probably wants to be alone.", she says, looking down at her feet.

I've never seen amber like this. Wait a minute. "Do you like Blaze?", I ask in a shocked, but really quiet voice. I don't want anyone inside to hear.

"NO. I just want to make sure he is okay. I care about him. As a teammate. Maybe even a friend. Reid was out of line. He shouldn't have said what he said. That's why I'm upset, okay? ", Amber says, trying to not make eye contact with me.

"Uh huh. You don't have to lie to me. Plus you would be good for Blaze and he would be good for you. You are both good friends, you already know you work well together, you know each other, and you actually genuinely care about him. When the battle is over and we all come back you need to tell him how you feel. You will never know if you don't try.", I say as I help Amber stand up.

"We'll see. But you better not say a word, got it?", she says in a serious tone.

"You have my word", I say, smiling to myself, as I open the door and go inside.

Chapter Nine
Amelia

It feels weird laying in bed after all the time that has passed. Since Sophia and her parents decided to leave after the first battle my mother was able to rearrange the rooms so that way Colin and I could have my room.

I might not have been as close with Sophia as some of my other family, but it still made me sad that they left. I understand why though. What we are doing is dangerous. Standing up against the Serpents is asking for trouble.

We know what we are getting ourselves into though. We have trained and studied together as a team for a long time. I know without a doubt that my family, Blaze, and his team will fight with everything that they have. I trust them with my life and I know Colin feels the same.

I can hear my father and Ace laughing and talking downstairs together. It reminds me of how he used to laugh with Joseph. I love hearing my father this way. He deserves to have a best friend again. It just hurts me for my mother. She doesn't seem very close to her sister. Her sister is so different from her. Chelsea is intense as a witch, wife, and mother. My mother is so calm and loving. Magic has always been something that we have fun doing that brings us together. But her sister's family sees magic as their defense. Which in our case is a good thing. Them being on our side in battle makes me feel better.

Everyone makes me feel strong though. So many of them have their own strengths. I know we are going to win. I can feel it. I believe in Colin, myself, my family, and in Blaze's team.

Stella and my relationship reminds me of my mother and Kate's. The day I turned sixteen Colin was still with Blaze. It was an awful time. I still don't like to think about it. Thinking of him being away from me for all that time makes my stomach hurt. Stella could tell when I woke up that morning that I had been crying that whole night. I sat down at the table and she abruptly got up and went outside. I was confused but I was too sad to question why. My mother and father ate breakfast with me as usual. I picked at my food until they were done eating.

I was about to get up from my seat and go back upstairs to lay down again, when Stella came through the front door with the biggest smile on her face. "What are you doing?", I asked her, in a shocked face. She comes over to me and wraps a blind fold around my eyes. "Wesley, Leah, and Hannah are going to meet you guys at the back door.", Stella said to my parents.

I could hear the excitement in my mothers voice. After a minute or two I heard the backdoor shut.

Stella grabbed my hand and led me to the front door. "No peeking", Stella said giggling. I was trying so hard not to trip over anything. I could feel my heart beating with excitement and the pit in my stomach growing from guilt.

I kept thinking that I didn't want a party. I wanted Colin. I wanted to hear his voice and his laugh. I wanted to feel his hand on my face and his lips pressed against mine.

I held on to Stellas hand as she led me around the house. Her hand was warm and I could hear laughing as she let go and started to untie the blindfold. "Keep your eyes closed until we say three okay? One, two, three!", she yelled in a happy and high pitched tone.

I opened my eyes to see picnics laid out for everyone. Stella had put out a blanket for each family. She sat me with my mom, my dad, and her. "I know I am your cousin, but in my heart you are my sister." Stella said, wrapping her arms around me.

I held her tight, "I love you so much. Thank you. You are my cousin, best friend, and sister all in one. I don't know what I would ever do without you.", I said, wiping my tears away.

"I knew you wouldn't want a party, so I decided an early birthday lunch would be the perfect way to celebrate, without celebrating.", Stella said, holding both my hands out in front of her, smiling at me.

I looked around at everyone sitting on their blankets. It meant the world to me. I couldn't wait for Colin to be with us and for everyone to meet him. I knew they would all love him as much as my parents and I do.

We all stayed outside together that day until the sun went down. It was so wonderful hearing everyone's stories, laughter, and making memories.

My favorite story that day was a story my grandmother told. Her and my grandfather were sitting on a blanket across from ours.

"It was a stormy night. The wind and rain was hitting our windows so hard that it sounded like they were going to break. I had just turned sixteen. I was at home with my mother, father, and my brother. I was grabbing extra blankets when I heard a knock at the door. I peered around the corner of the hallway to see who it was. I couldn't believe someone would be out in a storm. Then walked in the most beautiful man I had ever seen. That man was your grandfather. My father and brother immediately liked him and enjoyed his company. My mother was amazed by his manners, intelligence, and the fact that he was also a witch. My father sensed it as soon as he walked through the door. I wasn't interested in love though. I was always very good at magic and fearless. I wanted to save the world and show everyone what I could do.", my grandmother said, smiling at my grandfather.

"That's what made me fall in love with her. She never let anyone tell her she couldn't do something. She was and is the kindest, most caring soul I've ever met. But in the same breath she is like fire, ready to take on the world." my grandfather said looking into my grandmother's eyes.

They were so beautiful sitting there together. You could feel their love even after all the years they had been together. I had to look away. It made me miss Colin so much more.

I get out of bed and walk over to my mirror. I look at the person staring back at me. I have always judged my appearance so harshly. But when I look at others I see so many beautiful qualities. I rarely ever look at someone and see any physical flaws and yet I see nothing but flaws when I look at myself.

I run my hands down my waist, wishing that it would magically get smaller, wanting my thighs to not touch, and cringing at the sight of my face looking more round than normal.

"Don't do that.", Colin says, walking up behind me.

I jump, startled by his presence. "I didn't hear you come in.", I say, nervously pulling on the seam of my dress.

He rests his hands on my shoulders and then he runs his hands down my arms until he reaches my hands. He then intertwines his fingers into mine, stopping me from fiddling with my dress.

"If you could only see yourself the way I see you. Your green eyes are like the forest, making me feel at home. Your lips are so soft, the most beautiful shade of pink, and they always curl up in the cutest way when you smile or grin. I love the way you scrunch your nose up when you are reading or concentrating on something. I love your body. Every single inch of you is perfect. It blows my mind that you cannot see it. I mean look at yourself, love. Look.", he says, wrapping his arms around my waist.

I lean into him. I love the feeling of him standing behind me, holding me, and staring at me. I feel goosebumps starting to form on my arms and the little hairs sticking up.

"You think I am perfect?", I say shyly, looking back at him in the mirror.

"Amelia Jones, I think you are the sexiest woman that I have ever seen standing here in front of me. Perfect does not come close to describing you.", He says then he spins me around to face him.

He puts his finger underneath my chin, bringing my face to his. Our lips are touching but we are not kissing. "If I have to remind you every single day until I take my last breath that you are beautiful, I will. As long as there is even the smallest chance that you might one day believe me.", he whispers.

I do not say a word. I need his lips on mine. I close the space between us, making our lips meet. His hands move down my body and he grabs my waist. I love the way he smells of firewood from the fireplace and that he tastes like lemonade. I cling to him as tightly as he is holding on to me. I do not think we will ever get enough of each other. He claims my body like he claims my soul, my life, and my whole entire existence. My senses welcome him in, my body aches for his, and my mind is consumed by thoughts of him.

He pulls away, not even an inch from my face, ""I love you so much.", he whispers.

I smile as I whisper back to him, "I love you too. More than you will ever know."

"I think I have an idea of how much you love me."Colin says, winking at me.

"Oh do you now.", I say in a sarcastic tone.

"I think I do. I think you love me just as much as I love you. Only I love you just a little bit more.". He says with a grin.

I love the goofiness in his voice. He lets go of me and slowly moves over to the bed and sits down.

I do not move. I stay where I am standing just admiring him. His beautiful eyes, his sexy grin, the way his muscles show through his shirt, and the way he takes my breath away as he runs his fingers through his hair as he pushes it back out of his face. Seeing him sitting on my bed now makes me feel so grateful. Those years without him were so painful.

What is it love?"Colin asks..

"Oh nothing. I was just thinking about how sexy you are and how I never want to be without you ever again.", I say as I walk toward him.

Colin pulls me onto his lap and gently cups my face with his hands. "Being without you was like not being able to catch my breath. I barely felt alive. I never want to be apart from you like that either. I love you so much.", Colin says as he looks into my eyes. I can feel the pain and sincerity in his voice.

"I love you so much too. I don't know what I would have done without my parents and Stella. I felt so broken and alone without you. I am so happy that we are together again. I can't wait to be your wife.", I say.

Colin slowly pulls my face closer to his until our lips meet. You would think that after kissing him as many times as I have, that I wouldn't get so lost in it still. But I do. I can feel my heart racing. His tongue is wet as it glides across mine. I love him so much. Everything about him. Every touch makes me fall more and more in love with him.

I remove my mouth from his, I slowly kiss his cheek and neck. " We need to get some sleep. We have to get up first thing in the morning. You know Blaze will come in here himself to get us up if we are late." I say laughing.

Colin slowly moves his hands from my face all the way down to my hips. "I know. I know. I just can't help it. You are so beautiful.", he says, squeezing my hips. I let out a squeak, "Colin!", I say as I jump off his lap and on to the bed next to him.

Colin starts laughing hysterically, "what was that about?", he says barely being able to talk from laughing.

"It's not funny. We're being too loud.", I say laughing. I get out of bed and go over to the closet.

"My bag is on the floor next to the door if you want to wear one of my tshirts love?", Colin says.

I smile at him as I walk over to the bag. I take his shirt out and lay it on the bed. Without thinking I remove my clothes. I look up to see Colin staring at me. His eyes are filled with desire. He slowly moves from the top of the bed to the bottom. His movements are so quiet that I don't even hear him move. He grabs the t-shirt, pulls me so close that there is not even a centimeter of space between us. He kisses me so deep. The warmth of his lips sends shivers down my spine. My knees feel like they are going to give out any second.

He pulls the shirt over my head, tucks a strand of my hair behind my ear, and kisses me. This time there is a heat behind his kiss that I have never felt before. He reluctantly pulls away, "I can't wait for us to have our own place."he says looking deep into my eyes. I can't hide the big smile on my face.

I cannot wait for us to have our own place either. I want him just as much as he wants me.

He smiles as he pulls me onto the bed. The air catches in my throat as he slowly pulls his shirt over his head.

His body is perfect.

I grab the blanket and cover us up. Colin pulls me close to him and I lay my head on his chest. His heart's still beating so fast. "I would love to make love to you right now. But just getting to lay here with you like this is a gift.", Colin says

Stella slowly creaks the door open, "Do you guys have clothes on?"she asks giggling.

"Yes, we have clothes on.", I answer in a dramatic tone.

"I brought some snacks and some coloring books," Stella says.

We all lay in bed together, coloring, while we eat our weight in cookies, chips, and sour candies. Our conversations consist of all the things we want to do one day. Stella is so excited to be a mother. But she said she wants to be the cool aunt for at least five years while she travels back and forth. She wants to be a photographer.

I imagine rocking my sweet baby in my arms and Stella coming to visit. We lay on the couch together while she tells me all about the world and shows me her beautiful photos. I can see her glowing as she holds her Godchild. I have not told her yet, but I am going to ask her once that day comes. There is no one that I would trust more than her.

After a while we say goodnight and Stella leaves the room. I snuggle back into Colin, melting into his warm and strong arms.

I wake up to Colin with his arms still wrapped around me. I carefully move and get out of bed. I throw on a tshirt and a pair of leggings. I get one shoe on but I accidently drop the other one, causing him to wake up.

"I'm sorry babe, I didn't mean to wake you up. It is four in the morning. The sun is not even up yet. I am going to go out back and train in the forest for a couple hours before everyone gets up. You should get some rest. I can get you up when I get done if you'd like?",I say.

He sits up out of bed and says, "Nonsense. Give me a minute to throw some clothes on and I will train with you."

"Okay. That sounds great.", I say smiling.

He raises his arms up stretching trying to wake up. I pause tying my shoe to stare at him. He looks so beautiful with his messy hair, his sleepy eyes, and the sun coming through the window making his eyes look like two pools of water. Sparkling like a clear stream. He looks up at me smiling, catching me staring at him. "You are so handsome.", I say blushing.

He walks over to me, placing his hand on my hip and pulling me close to him. I giggle as he uses his other hand to lift me up off of the floor. "You are perfect from your head to your toes.", Colin says with a silly voice.

He kisses my lip slowly and gently sits me down. Colin bends down and grabs my shoes. My heart skips a beat as he pulls the shoe onto my foot. He takes his time tying it. He then looks up at me. His smile is the most beautiful thing I have ever seen. "Thank you", I say smiling.

"Anything for you love. I am going to grab some clothes and jump in the shower. I will meet you outside.", Colin says.

"Okay. I love you." I say then I stand on my tiptoes to kiss Colin. He normally bends down to meet me halfway. I feel so short compared to him. I am only five foot three. He is six foot. I think it is cute that he is so much taller than me though.

He picks me up playfully and throws me on the bed, climbs on top of me, and starts tickling me. "Stop, you have to go get ready! Please!", I say laughing uncontrollably.

"Okay, okay. But only because you said please.", He says then he places his lips on mine. My chest is still rising and falling quickly from laughing so much. His touch makes goosebumps rise on my arms. I know we need to stop so he can get ready, but I just love the feeling of his body so close to mine. The way he smells, tastes, and feels takes over me.

Colin pushes off the bed to stand up. "I really am going to get in the shower this time.", he says laughing as he walks to the door. He smiles back at me before opening the door and leaves. I am taken back by every move he makes. Everyday I do not think that I can love him anymore than I already do. Then the next day comes and I fall even more in love with him. He is just so romantic, kind, and silly. I love the way he makes me laugh and how alive I feel when I am in his presence. I fall for him more and more each day.

Chapter Ten

Colin

I turn the shower on and feel the warm water wash over me. I hurry as I wash my hair and body. I know Amelia is probably already outside waiting on me. I turn the water off and get out of the shower. My towel is soft and smells like lavender. Grace always makes all the laundry smell so good.

Today I am wearing a charcoal gray t-shirt, blue jeans, and my boots. I quietly walk downstairs and out the back door.

I see Amelia talking to Stella, Hannah, Luke, Troy, and Oliver.

"I didn't expect everyone to be up so early."I say, as I walk toward them.

"Hannah and I come out this early to train every morning!"Wesley says in an enthusiastic voice as he runs past me to stand with the others.

"I have never slept past five. My mother and father always say there is too much to learn and do to sleep the morning away.", Hannah says in a serious voice.

"It sounds like you could use some fun.", Troy says with a smirk.

Hanna looks shocked but I can see her cheeks start to turn pink as she looks down. "Maybe one day,"she says.

"So, what do you guys want to do first?"Amelia asks.

"Let's play freeze tag!"Wesley says.

"Raise your hand if you have played before", Amelia says.

Hannah, Amelia, Wesley, and I raise our hands.

Okay. Well the rules are really simple. You try to be the last one standing. You can only freeze your opponents with the statue spell, not an actual ice spell. You cannot use any other spells to disarm, hurt, or cheat your opponents. If someone is casting a spell at you and you catch them you can block it. Everyone understand?"Amelia says.

"Oooh this will be easy!"Oliver says. "Don't be so sure. I have been playing this game since I was a kid. I never lose", Stella says cheerfully.

Oliver winks at Stella and says, "We'll see.".

I walk over to Amelia to give her a kiss before we start the game. I lift her up with one arm. She giggles as we kiss and I sit her down. "Go easy on me." I say to her,

"Never.", she says back at me smiling.

We all go to separate ends of the backyard. "One more thing! You have to stay on the ground. No flying, going up trees, or hiding in the treehouse.", Amelia says.

"Got it!"Everyone says together.

"Ready, Set, Go!"Stella yells.

I go over to one of the big trees next to our treehouse and hide behind it. I see Luke across the yard sneaking up behind Hannah. She smiles and turns around before he can raise his wand."Got you!", she yells as she casts the spell, freezing him.

I laugh to myself. She is good. Oliver and Troy are battling close to the house. It is getting intense. Troy is so focused and looks really serious. Oliver on the other hand is laughing and having fun.

Hannah comes out of nowhere and starts attacking them both. "What happened to having fun?" She says to Troy.

"I am. But I also plan on winning", Troy says confidently. Never breaking his focus.

"Oh really." Hannah says, then she casts a spell that shoots right past Troy's head. He barely moves in time in order for it to not hit him.

I can see him clench his wand tightly. I focus on Oliver and cast a spell freezing him right as he was about to get Troy. Now it is even and Hannah and Troy can properly battle it out. They both look in my direction but then they quickly go back to battling each other.

I hear a branch snap behind me. I block the spell coming at me as fast as I can. I look to see that it is Wesley. I start firing off spell after spell trying to get him. But he is a lot faster than he looks. I bob and weave in between the trees. He must be hiding because I can no longer see him. I sneak around the trees trying to catch him.

The wind blows and the leaves scatter across the ground. I listen closely to the world around me. I hear rustling above me. It is a squirrel jumping onto another tree. The earthy smell of the dirt and leaves consumes my nose. I look closely at each tree around me. Out of the corner of my eye I see the top of Wesley's shoe poking out behind a tree. I sneak toward him. I pick up a branch and throw it in the opposite direction next to him. He moves out from behind the tree and I immediately strike him.

So that means Wesley, Oliver, and Luke are out of the game. I hear the sound of laughing and people running towards the house. I see Troy and Hannah still battling each other. But I can tell that Hannah is definitely winning and getting the best of Troy. He is starting to look tired and is losing his focus. But he looks happy. They both do.

I can see Amelia standing next to our treehouse smiling as she watches them. I love how much she loves her family and how she has always enjoyed the happiness of others.

"Are you ready to lose?"Hannah says to Troy, taunting him.

"Would you really freeze me?", he says flirting with her.

"Of course I would. I am the most competitive person playing this game right now. I would freeze my own parents to win.". She says laughing.

I know she is being funny, but I can tell she is serious. Hannah is unlike anyone I have ever met. She is so intelligent and calculated. It is like she doesn't speak or do anything without thinking it through first. Troy moves toward her. I think they're going to kiss. My jaw drops, I stand at the edge of the trees in shock. Hannah is smiling as she goes to move toward him as well. Troy's lips are so close to hers. All of sudden she pulls back and strikes him.

I gasp not being able to believe what I just witnessed. Technically she didn't break any rules so she didn't cheat. I think laughing to myself. Hannah starts running toward the treehouse. I look in the direction where Amelia was standing a moment ago, but now she is gone.

I quickly look around trying to spot her. But it's like she has vanished. I move back into the woods more trying to blend in with the trees. I breathe in right as the wind blows. I smell Amelia's perfume. She must be close to me.

I bend down as I start to walk into the woods again. The smell of Amelia's perfume is getting stronger and stronger. I see Stella hiding behind a large bush. She is watching Hannah. She is actually in a really good hiding spot. I think she has a chance at getting her. I wave at her getting her attention. She spots me and her eyes go wide. "I'm not going to freeze you. I'll help you get Hannah.", I whisper.

She gives me a thumbs up. I look up to see Hannah no longer standing where she was. Stella notices it right as I do. We both look at each other with worry because we know she has spotted one of us. Before I can take a step I feel Hannah behind me. I don't even try to move.

I know she's got me.

Chapter Eleven

Amelia

It is just a game I repeat to myself as I watch Colin turn into a statue. I tried so hard to get to him before Hannah struck him, but I was too late.

I move toward Hannah slowly trying to not let her see me. The moment Stella saw Hannah behind Colin she ran the other way to hide. I need to find her.

Hannah is so fast. She runs through the trees like she knows every branch, rock, and bump on the ground. I have ran through this forest since I can remember, and I can't even move that well in here.

I lose track of her. She has to be close there is no way that she could have gotten far. I was just behind her. I am close to the stream. I can hear the water flowing. I have always loved the sound of it.

I see Stella running toward me, but I do not think she can see me. Hannah spots her too. I start running toward her, but she is still so far away from me. I move to the tree line to get a better shot at hitting Hannah, but I still can't get a good enough shot. She casts trying to hit Stella, right as I get close enough to hit her. I don't have time to cast the spell, so I jump in front of her taking the hit for Stella.

I wake up on my back on the ground. The grass is cool beneath me. "Why did you do that?!"Stella asks.

"I pinky promised that I would always have your back. Remember?", I say, smiling at her.

"Always.", She says in a bubbly voice as she wraps her pinky around mine.

"So what do I get for winning?"Hannah says.

"You didn't get her?!" I say to Stella, in a shocked voice.

"I was in shock that you took the hit for me! Sorryyyy.". Stella says laughing.

Colin walks toward me. He grabs my hand to help me stand up. I smile up at him. "I think you did great love.", he says as he pulls me to my feet.

"You didn't do so bad yourself.", I say, winking at him.

"Is it just me or did someone have fun?"Troy says, taunting Hannah.

"I always have fun when I win, and I always win." Hannah says back to him with a flip of her hair as she walks back towards the house. Troy shakes his head at all of us with a smile, then he walks towards the house after her.

But he doesn't walk too fast. So that way she doesnt think that he is rushing after her. Those two are impossible. It is obvious that they are head over heels for one another. They are both just too stubborn to admit it. "They are so cute", Stella says in a bubbly voice.

"What are you talking about?"Wesley asks Stella.

"Isn't it obvious? Hannah and Troy are totally falling for each other.", Stella says, answering him.

"Yeah right. The only thing Hannah might fall for is a book. All she does is study. I am surprised she even knows any of our names.", Wesley says.

"That is a little harsh don't you think? You can be focused on your studies and still be friendly."Blaze says out of nowhere. We all jump at the same time at the sound of his voice.

"I didn't mean to come off as harsh. I really like Hannah. I just didn't think she was capable of liking someone.", Wesley says in a nervous voice.

"Everyone is capable of falling in love.", Stella says, batting her eyes.

"Especially when the girl is as pretty as you." Oliver says, wrapping his arm around Stella. Her face turns bright pink. I am pretty sure she is going to faint any second.

"You're…. You're so sweet.", Stella stutters back to Oliver.

"Well it looks like all of you have had enough fun this morning. You guys should go eat breakfast. Seth has something he wants to say to everyone after we eat and then we are all going to meet back out here. After that everyone can get cleaned up and then we're going to hit the road." Blaze says in his serious voice. He looks off into the forest. I can tell he is worried.

Colin grabs my hand and pulls it to his lips. He kisses my hand gently, "everything is going to be okay love.", he says sweetly.

I normally would feel safe and comforted by his words and affection, but for some reason I am still filled with so much worry. I cannot shake this feeling that I have that something terrible is about to happen.

Chapter Twelve

Colin

I can sense uneasiness from Amelia. I wish that I could ease her mind, but I know once she gets a bad feeling there is nothing I can do to make it go away. I gently rub her hand as we sit at the table together. Her mother has made french toast, fruit salad, eggs, and sausage.

Normally Amelia loves the sound of the dishes clanking, everyone talking, the laughter, and everyone filling their bellies. But this morning it is like she is sitting here with us, but she is not really here.

"Is there anything I can do for you love?", I whisper to her. She doesn't budge.

"Amelia…, love.., darling?", I say, trying to get her attention.

She finally looks at me with concerned eyes, "Oh sorry. I was just thinking. I know it is not going to be easy. But this feeling I am getting, it's more than just worry. I am scared, for all of us.", she says, with great fear in her voice and eyes

I grab ahold of her hand and squeeze it tight, "We all have each other. Everything is going to be okay.", I whisper back to her. She gives me a weak smile and leans her head on my shoulder.

Amelia's father stands up from the table, "We will be meeting with my mother tomorrow. I know she will have a plan and we can all add to it when we get there. But for now I need everyone to continue training and studying like normal. If you are unsure about something or you need help with a specific spell myself, Blaze, Ace, and both of Hannah's parents have volunteered to assist. Do not hesitate to ask one of us for help. We all need to be at a hundred percent when we challenge the serpents. I know it is scary and we do not know what is going to happen. But we know each other and we know ourselves. Rely on the person next to you as much as you rely on yourself. We are a team.", he says in the most serious tone. I've never seen him so stern, but somehow calm.

When I look at Seth and I think of my father I get this feeling of hope. I want to be a good leader like them. They both have taught me so much about strength, knowledge, and love. I want nothing more than to be as good as man as they are.

"Everyone needs to meet in the backyard in ten minutes. We are going to do a training exercise. It is mandatory.", Blaze says. He gets up from the table and goes out the back door.

"Do you think we will be on teams?"Stella says to Amelia and I excitedly.

"I hope so. That would be so fun.", Amelia answers back. Her face looks more relaxed and she is smiling. I breathe a sigh of relief. Hopefully this training with everyone is just what she needs to get this bad feeling out of her head.

"If we get to be on teams I will pick you guys! I am going to go find Oliver. I will meet you guys outside.", Stella says and then she skips away.

"I wish I had her energy.", I say laughing.

"I think everyone does.", Amelia says giggling. We stand up from the table together and go into the backyard to wait on everyone else.

"Thanks to a brilliant idea from Stella, I have put everyone on teams. Before I tell you guys what teams you are on I have something I want to say. Have fun. I know the next few days are going to be serious and some moments are going to be very scary, so I want this moment to be good. Anyways, the first team is going to be Blaze, Carol, Colin, Amelia and Stella. The next team will be myself, Jack, Alice, Jane, and

Luke. Then Seth, Amber, Wyatt, Troy, and Leah. Next is Chelsea, Ace, Oliver, Wesley, Hannah. Then Zeke, Reid, and Henry will be the healing group.You can only be healed once. George and Rick will be keeping score. Xavier and Beth will be the referees. Martin will be on the side lines for anyone to tap in if they need a break, but remember in real battle there won't be anyone there to tap in." Grace says.

On the count of three, find your teammates. "One... two.. Three! You have two minutes to discuss a game plan. Your time starts..now!"Xavier yells.

"We should spit up.", Blaze says.

"What? The whole part of being a team is sticking together?" Stella pouts.

"Yeah I agree with Stella. If we work together and use all of our strengths as one, we can win!"Amelia says eagerly.

I smile at her with pride.

"Yeah, okay. What is your plan then?"Blaze says to Amelia.

She looks taken back. She definitely does not have a plan. I chuckle to myself. She nudges me playfully.

"Okay so I am good at throwing things. I can be at the edge of the forest launching logs at people with my levitating spell. Carol can be gathering logs for me to throw. Stella, you can be keeping an eye on the ball for any openings to grab it. Blaze and Colin, you guys can be taking out everyone that comes near Stella and I.", She says confidently.

"So Blaze and I are bodyguards? Cool", I say chuckling.

Amelia smiles as she rolls her eyes at me.

"Sounds like a plan. Oh and Grace made me promise to say this.. Have fun.", Blaze mumbles.

We all burst out into laughter.

"Was that so hard to say?"Stella says in a bubbly voice to Blaze.

"Just focus on us winning.", Blaze says back to her with a sarcastic smile.

Blaze and I take position in front of Amelia and Stella.

"The goal is to keep the ball of ice from touching the ground.

But that is not the hard part. The hard part is trying to keep it from touching the ground while your teammates are attacking you and trying to get the ball. You are not allowed to try to break the ice ball or change the element of the ball. If you are caught going out of bounds you will immediately be kicked out of the game. No going into the forest, in the house, or in the tree house. Once you are the last team standing, get the ice ball and raise it above your head. Then I will announce you as the winner. It is time to begin. On your marks, get set, GO!"Xavier yells.

Xavier shoots a wave of water up in the air and freezes it into a ball. Without hesitation Hannah elevates herself into the air and catches it. Troy tries to throw a chunk of the yard up at her, but Wesley explodes it and the ground below Troy. The blow causes him to get launched across the yard. For a split second I see a look of panic shoot across Hannah's face as she looks in Troy's direction. But she quickly regains her concentration.

She throws it to Wesley. Jane and Alice put their hands together. They then turn, exposing both of their hands towards Wesley. A big gush of water comes blasting out of their hands, causing him to fall over.

The ice ball goes flying into the air. I make eye contact with Amelia. She knows exactly what I am thinking. She levitates logs off the ground for me to jump on like steps until I am high enough in the air to grab the ball.

I shoot Amelia a smile as I snatch the ball and pass it to Blaze. Amelia and Stella start shooting ice at everyone coming towards Blaze. He throws it back into the air towards me. Before I can catch it Troy makes a gust of wind that shoots the ball across the yard into Amber's hands.

Troy and Jack go back and forth attacking each other. I can see Beth keeping an eye on them to make sure things don't get out of hand.

The amusement in Jack's face from the effort that Troy is putting into his attacks makes me laugh. Jack does not seem phased at all.

"Is that all you got?"Jack says, laughing. Troy does not look like he thinks Jack's words are funny.

Ace and Chelsea cast a sheet of ice underneath Leah and Seth. They slip and slide, trying to catch their balance. They crash to the ground with a burst of laughter.

Amber tries to quickly throw the ball to Wyatt as she races across the yard, but Hannah is already two steps ahead of her; she fires a blow at Wyatt causing him to be out of the game. He had already been healed once from a blow from Jane.

Hannah catches the ball. Amelia shoots past me colliding with her. They both go crashing to the ground. Before hitting the ground Hannah throws the ball into the air. Grace leaps over Hannah and Blaze snatching the ball. Amelia stands up quickly to highfive Blaze, but Hannah, filled with rage, shoves passed Amelia. "Another move like that Hannah, and you're out of the game!"Xavier yells.

"Sorry.", Hannah says ro Amelia. Trying to be sincere but also trying to get back to the game. "I understand. It's okay.", Amelia says laughing as she hugs Hannah.

Hannah hugs her back and then darts off to catch up to Blaze.

I love my girl's kindness. She makes me see the good in people, she makes me hope, and realize that being angry is a choice.

She chooses to be nice even when she is shown the opposite.

"You know you are Amazing right?", I whisper into her ear.

She leans her head back into my chest and then tilts her head to look back at me, "Not as amazing as you.", she says and gives me a quick kiss.

I look up to see that Zeke is healing Leah, Beth is leading Jane to sit next to Wyatt for going out of bounds, and Stella has the ball. Blaze must have passed it to her while Amelia and I were talking.

Hannah and Troy are right on her heels. They're both fighting with each other as they chase after Stella.

Troy is laughing while hitting Hannah with balls of water. Hanna is laughing along with him as she counter attacks him, sending the balls of water back into his face. They are obviously having a blast drenching each other in water.

Blaze and Carol are running to the other end of the yard. Stella looks to Blaze to throw it to him and then to Carol. I can tell she wants to get rid of the ball as quickly as she can.

The nervousness on her face is so funny. I have never seen her run so fast. "Blaze help me!", she yells. Blaze looks at me with the biggest smile on his face. It makes me so happy to see him enjoying himself.

Amelia moves so quickly past Stella that it takes me a moment to even process that she moved. She takes the ball from Stella and yells, "I got your back!"

Stella laughs as she sticks her pinky finger up in the air. She then bends over with her hands on her knees and very dramatically breathes out a gust of air.

Amelia then throws the ball to Carol.

At this point Ace has taken out Alice and Chelsea. Oliver has taken out Amber, Wesley, and he almost has Jack.

All of sudden Jack gets a surge of energy. Electricity moves through his hands and out of his fingertips. He attacks Oliver causing him to be launched out of bounds.

"You're out Jack for excessive force and Oliver you are out for being out of bounds."

"Worth it."Jack says laughing. I Shake his hand before he goes to sit on the sidelines.

"Here is a quick head count. On team Blaze everyone is left., On team Grace Alice, Jane, and Jack are out. Team Seth has lost Amber and Wyatt. Lastly, Chelsea's team has lost Chelsea and Oliver. So we have Blaze, Carol, Stella, Amelia, Colin, Grace, Seth, Troy, Leah, Ace, Wesley, and Hannah!", George yells.

Amelia runs, throwing the ball to Carol. But Carol runs too far trying to catch the ball and goes out of bounds.

Hannah of course catches the ball. She gives Troy a taunting grin. I go after Hannah. My breath gets louder as I move faster and faster. Blaze follows behind me.

Troy with a look of frustration goes after Ace and Wesley. He casts blow after blow at them. His attacks go from water to fire. I lose focus watching the look in his eyes. Something about Troy seems off to me. I can't put my finger on it. Hannah is obviously competitive. But Troy doesn't seem to care about the game. He cares about showing his strength. Like proving he is stronger than us.

Wesley tries to make him lose his balance by making cracks in the ground behind him as he runs, but it does not phase Troy.

Ace goes down with a fire spell from Troy. Then Wesley almost immediately after. The burn marks on their arms and legs are quickly healed by Henry as they walk away.

They do not seem phased at all by Troy's attacks as they laugh together. Maybe I am just overthinking Troy's actions. I am going to keep an eye on him for now. I just do not want to hurt Amber's feelings by questioning or having doubts about him.

Troy then tries to go after Hannah but is stopped by Blaze.

Troy laughs at him, "What are you going to do?" he says with a sarcastic tone.

"Don't underestimate me. Remember that I have a lot of years and experience on you.", Blaze says back to him.

"I am not underestimating you. I just know that you are not a challenge. My power exceeds far beyond my age.", Troy says with a smirk.

Troy casts spell after spell, but Blaze blocks every one. Sweat runs down Troy's face as he tries to keep up. Seth and Leah jump in to help Troy, but Blaze immediately takes out Leah. Troy takes advantage of Blaze being distracted with Seth to run after Hannah.

Amelia and I trap Hannah in between us. I hear Rick yell that Seth is out of the game. Blaze must have got him.

Stella is running from Grace. I can tell she wants to be out of the game. I cannot help laughing at her. With her eyes closed Stella casts a spell at Grace. She hits the ground. Stella slowly opens her eyes.

Filled with pride and excitement she starts jumping up and down.

Unfortunately she is so distracted by her excitement that she does not see Troy coming up behind her. Blaze makes his way in between Stella and Troy knocking him to the ground. Troy's face turns bright red.

His eyes narrow. But then his eyes meet mine. He knows I am watching him.

Hannah shoots fire at Stella taking her out of the game, right before Amelia can snatch the ball from her.

Stella doesn't seem upset though. She dances the whole way to sit with everyone else. Amelia sees her and starts dancing too. Hannah shoots Amelia in the back. But thankfully she has not been healed yet.

Zeke heals her, but right as she gets healed Troy hits her. Amelia just smiles and walks to sit next to Stella.

This is supposed to be fun, so we're going to show him how it is done.

I shoot Blaze a smile and he nods his head. He blocks Troy from getting to me.

I run after Hannah throwing pieces of the ground at her. "Come on Hannah, why are you running?", I yell laughing.

"Run? From you? Never!"Hannah yells back to me with a smile.

We each start levitating pieces of the ground into the air. We go up and up, throwing ice, water, and dirt at each other. The ball goes back and forth between us.

BOOM!

The ground shakes. We both lose concentration and go crashing to the ground. I quickly grab the ball and hold on tight.

I regain focus and see that Blaze and Troy are standing in a puff of smoke. They are both trying to catch their breath.

Blaze lifts his hand and hits Troy with one last blow. Blaze stands all the way up as he helps him to his feet. "You did good man. You fought a good fight.", Blaze says to Troy.

Unfortunately Troy scoffs under his breath as he walks away.

I feel a shot to my side. Reid heals me but Hannah is too quick. She's got me. I walk out of the game behind troy. All that is left now is Blaze and Hannah. Hannah looks like she has already won by the smile on her face.

She throws the ball in the air as far as she can. It is like all of her movements are happening in slow motion. Blow after blow she hits Blaze with everything she has. He blocks every attack, not taking even a second to look up at the ball.

The ball is starting to come back down. Hannah is still not letting up on her attacks. Blaze lifts one arm into the air, still blocking with the other. He catches the ball and sends it right back up into the air. Just as the ball leaves his hand he blasts a shot at Hannah.She gets launched back with not a single warning. Before she can get healed or stand up he hits her again. Taking her out. Without looking Blaze raises his arm back up and catches the ball.

Everyone goes WILD. "GO BLAZE!", I scream. Amelia, Stella, and I run to Blaze, wrapping him in a group hug. Carol walks over to join us too. "We did it!"Stella yells in a high pitched voice.

"Technically, I did it.", Blaze says sarcastically .

With all the excitement going on around me, I look over to see Troy helping Hannah up. She looks hypnotized. Like the whole world around her is gone. She has lost, but for the first time, she does not care.

Chapter Thirteen

Amelia

It takes a little over three hours to get to Waynesville. I have always wondered what my parents' hometown looked like. Colin has never mentioned wanting to see it or anything. He has always been so content with living on our road.

I wish it was better circumstances bringing me to where my parents grew up. The hair on my arms stand up at the thought of seeing Ethan again. There is something so cold and weary about him.

There is no doubt that he is evil, but it is more than that. It is like he has no feeling but anger surrounding him.

I can only imagine the torment of never feeling any love or peace.

"We're riding with Blaze!"Stella yells as she runs up to me with her bag.

"Awe okay! I will sit in the middle so I can sit next to you and Colin.", I say smiling.

"I call shotgun then.", Amber says trying to hide her smile as she throws her bag in the trunk.

I see Colin talking to Blaze on the porch. The concentration on his face worries me. I wish Blaze would wait until they get in the car to make a game plan.

My dad honking his horn makes me jump! "We love you honey.

Blaze said we are all meeting at a campsite before we meet your grandmother. We will see you there. We love you!"my mother yells out her window.

"Okay, I love you guys too!" I yell back.

I watch everyone getting into eachothers cars. I love that my parents are letting Troy and Hannah ride with them. My dad and Ace are going to enjoy talking on the car ride. I can see my mom in the passenger seat daydreaming out the window while they talk about whatever men talk about it. Then Troy and Hannah will go back and forth in the back seat with Ace, flirting and arguing about who's stronger. Ace won't pay them any attention.

Blaze and Colin get in the car. Everyone is behind us in their cars. We're all set.

"We are going to stop at a campground that is just a few minutes outside Waynesville. We will wait there until my grandmother meets us. Then we will all figure out a plan to defeat the serpents once and for all.", Blaze says.

Blaze picks up Shadow and lays him behind his neck like a pillow as he sits in the driver seat. I can hear Shadow's purring from the back seat.

I rest my head on Colin's shoulder as we start our journey. I try not to dwell on what may come, but the future's so unpredictable that in this moment it is hard not to.

Of course Colin senses my uneasy thoughts and squeezes my hand. Even though it is a small gesture it still calms my nerves.

I look up into his eyes and smile. He places a kiss on my forehead and he pauses before he pulls away, "I love you Amelia Jones. Everything is going to be okay."

"I hope so. I just want to keep everyone safe. A million plans keep flooding my mind. I just do not know how to protect everyone at once.", I say worriedly.

Stella's arms wrapping around me startle me, "You will have me by your side the whole time. I've got your back.", Stella says smiling.

"I know you do. I'm not worried about myself. It's everyone else. I just can't imagine anyone getting hurt.", I say leaning into Stella.

"That is the price of war. No matter how small a battle might be, there will always be sacrafices.", Amber says bluntly.

"A little dark there don't you think?"Stella says, looking like she might vomit.

Blaze must have been looking through his rear view mirror the whole time because he chuckles.

"Like I was saying, everything is going to be okay.", Colin says sternly.

I see a look of concern in Blaze's eyes. He knows more than anyone what war can do. He was once a Serpent. He knows what they are capable of and what they can do.

He must be so worried for all of us. But I do not sense that from him. If anything I sense confidence in us from him.

I am confident in our family and friends too. I know we can do this. I will do everything within my power to protect everyone.

I love them and they need me to be at my strongest. We arrive at the campsite. The drive wasn't so bad. Stella sang every song that came on the radio. I enjoyed giggling at Blaze's obvious discomfort.

The campsite is beautiful. I get out behind Colin as he goes towards the trunk to get stuff out. I then head to the cabin area. I stop for a moment as the wind blows. The leaves around me are moving so fast in the breeze. The sound of trees swaying is like music bringing peace into my soul. The best part is the coolness in the air and the way it smells.

Colin intertwines his fingers in mine. I love how he utters not a word and joins me in the peaceful moment.

The moment is interrupted by Blaze barking orders at everyone. Colin and I laugh together at the list of demands.

We wait patiently to hear our names called.

"Stella, you're on Shadow duty!"Blaze yells.

"Really?! Me?"Stella jumps with excitement.

"Colin, Amelia, Troy, Hannah, Wesley, you all will go around and set up tents for everyone. There needs to be four people to six people in a tent. If you brought your own and want to sleep alone or you want less people then you need to tell one of them. If Seth, Carol, or myself provided the tent then be prepared to sleep with four to six people. I will be setting up my own tent, so mark me off your list Amelia."

I love how Blaze knew that I was making a list in my head the moment he gave us the job. I nod to him to let him know that I got it.

"Once everyone gets their tasks please let me know if you have your own tent.", I say.

"Troy and I can start setting up the tents.". Wesley says with enthusiasm.

Troy looks annoyed at being volunteered.

"I could always blow you up?"Wesley says to Troy, laughing.

Troy just rolls his eyes. But I know that Wesley really would if he starts to complain.

"Coming", Hannah says without asking as she follows behind Wesley and Troy.

"What would you like me to do love?", Colin asks me. He strokes my face slowly as he waits for my answer. The fire and passion in his eyes makes my knees weak.

"I brought a tent for just us. You can go ahead and get it set up if you'd like?, I ask with a flirtatious smile.

"Oh really?", he says, smiling ear to ear. He pulls me in for a kiss. I sway back and forth in his arms as he raises me off the ground.

I feel like I have constant butterflies in my stomach. Like the rollercoaster of our love never goes down. It just keeps going up. Maybe it is not a rollercoaster after all. Our love is like a waterfall. We pour into each other like a river pouring into the waterfall.

We support each other, comfort one another, we trust with no doubt, we love unconditionally, our affection is passionate, and our need for one another is loud. I am lost in his touch and I never want to be found.

He then sits me down and winks at me before walking away. I smile at the feeling of his touch still lingering on my skin.

The first team to come to me is Ace, Amber, Blaze, George, Xaveir, and Zeke. Their task is to gather the wood for the fire.

Everyone will be in the tent together except Blaze. "Aren't you claustrophobic?. I say to Amber, moving my eyebrows up and down.

I noticed Amber not being able to keep her eyes off of Blaze in the car. They would be perfect together.

She looks at me with confusion. Then realizes what I am doing and shakes her head no. I proceed anyway, "Blaze, is there room in your tent for one more?". I say trying to hint at him.

Blaze makes eye contact with me and then I gesture to Amber. He then looks a little stunned by my idea but I can tell he doesn't want to say no. "Yeah.. I guess. I don't want you to be uncomfortable. Uh yeah just bring your sleeping bag." Blaze says to Amber stuttering.

For a moment I think I am seeing things when Amber starts to blush. "Yeah I'll meet you at your tent after dinner.", Amber says quickly, then she walks away to start gathering firewood.

My grandpa, Jack, Carol, my mom, and my dad have the task of building the fire. They all are going to share a tent together.

Stella, Oliver, and Alice, Leah, Jane, and Wyatt are the next team. They are in charge of cooking dinner. Except Stella, she'll just be sharing a tent with them.

Beth and Henry will be in charge of gathering blankets and pillows. They'll be sharing a tent.

Reid and Martin are in charge of setting a barrier around our campsite. They will be sharing a tent together.

Once everyone's tasks are complete we all sit around the fire and eat hot dogs together. After we get done eating the parents get up and the rest of us stay sitting. I think we all want to get to know each other more.

"What did you guys do as kids? Did any of you live close to each other?", I ask, trying to not sound so curious.

"I think all of us just seen each other on the holidays. Except you and your family. We just thought you guys stayed to yourself.", Wesley says.

Hannah stands up with Troy, "I am on your mom's side so I do not have much knowledge on this discussion. Plus you know all about my life. All my family does is train. We will see you guys in the morning.", she says to me smiling and then they walk away.

Colin squeezes my hand, sensing my nerves. "We always knew we would all be together one day though."Stella says excitedly.

"I just, now that I know all of you I can't imagine not being in your lives. Can we make a pact to all stay in contact once the battle is over?" I ask.

Everyone starts saying yes or of course at the same time. It makes me so happy to see that I am not the only one that is really going to miss everyone.

"I don't think any of us could go back to the way it was before. I hope we can all move close together. We were all kind alone before. Now we are a real family.", Leah says.

"Exactly. We need each other.", I say.

I see my dad stepping out of his tent. "I am going to see if my dad will take a walk with me. I'll be back.". I whisper to Colin.

"Okay love. I'll finish talking with everyone. I love you.", he whispers back to me.

"I love you too.", I whisper, then I stand up and start walking towards my dad.

"Hey can we take a walk?", I say as I catch up with him.

"Of course honey. Are you okay?", he says with concern in his eyes.

"I'm okay. I just want to ask you a few questions." I say slowly.

"About what?", he says looking even more concerned.

"Why did we never go around the rest of our family? Even Chelsea, mom's sister. We never even visited. Why?" I ask nervously.

I'm starting to get cold. The wind is picking up. I cling to my jacket, trying to keep the heat in. My dad takes a deep breath in. For a second I think he might not say anything at all.

"If it wasn't for Joseph and Kate, your mother and I would have never taught you magic at all.", he says pausing, letting me process his words.

He can tell I am speechless, "It's not that your mother and I do not love magic, we do. It is that we came from families that made it who they were. Your mothers family was like her sister. All they did was train and study. There was no fun or joy in it. It was only to become stronger. Not being close with my family was very hard. You can see yourself that they are amazing. But my parents also really value their training. I wanted to do good with my magic but I decided when your mother found out that she was pregnant that I wanted more for you. You were not going to grow up with the expectation of saving people, just because you knew you had magic. We were shocked when Joseph and Kate felt the same way. We wanted to love you guys above anything else. But they also loved magic and wanted to share that with you guys. So we agreed. We all tried our very best to protect you guys from everything. Your mother will never forgive herself.", My father says sadly.

"What do you mean?" I ask, starting to worry.

My father studies the sky for a minute, "When you and Colin were born your mother didnt sleep. She was terrified of something or someone coming in to hurt one of us. So every night she would cast a spell around our houses. Joseph and Kate never picked on your mother about it. They loved that she protected everyone with it. Especially when you guys started sleeping in the treehouse.", he says.

"So that's why you guys never fought us on sleeping out there!" I say.

"Exactly.", he sighs. I realize what he is saying. I look up at him with so much sadness.

"Your mother did not put the force field up the night Joseph and Kate came home. We had fallen asleep. Them being killed that night shattered her heart. To this day she has not forgiven herself.", my father says, his voice wavering.

"But it's not her fault.", I say, starting to cry.

"Deep down your mother knows that. But she thinks that life is about choices and decisions. Once you do it you can never take it back. That's why she tried so hard to give you a safe and happy life. But we made choices that hurt you. We kept you from your family. Our houses weren't just there. We made them with magic. You and Colin's life was built on keeping you guys safe and hidden from the world. We thought by building you guys a perfect life that no harm would ever be able to get to you guys. But we were wrong.", he says, his words slowly coming to a whisper.

I wrap my arms around him, "You were an amazing father. Colin and I have the best parents. I would have done the same thing. I love you so much.", I say crying.

"Thank you honey. We really did try our best. We all loved you both so much.". He says sniffling.

We let go and start heading back to the tents. I just keep thinking about how hard our parents tried to protect us. I see Colin stand up. "It's okay. I am glad you came to talk with me. I love you. Go ahead and spend time with Colin.", My father says.

I give him another big hug, " I love you too. I am so proud to be your daughter.", I say letting go.

I watch my father walk to his tent. It feels as if a giant weight has been lifted off my shoulders. I understand our parents more, our life, our childhood, everything. It was all out of love. I knew my parents were protective. Joseph and Kate were too. They really did everything they could.

Chapter Fourteen

Colin

I sense mixed feelings as I approach Amelia. "Is everything okay?", I ask.

"Yes I just needed some questions answered. I'll tell you all about it in the morning, I promise. But for right now I would love to lay down." She says, letting me pull her into my arms.

"Of course love. I'll lead the way.", I say.

I walk a good distance into the woods away from everyone else. Amelia's silent confusion makes me smile. I love the way she lights up at our tent next to the lake.

"I wanted tonight to be special", I say.

"Oh it is. It is perfect.", she says overjoyed.

We walk hand in hand into our tent. I have our sleeping bags laid out on the ground with petals scattered everywhere. I also made sure to grab a bunch of pillows.

The lit lanterns at the corners of the tent are so bright. "Would you like me to turn down the lanterns love?", I ask.

"Just a little bit.", she says smiling.

I love the look in her eyes. "Go ahead and lay down love. I am going to turn down the lanterns", I say. I turn down the last lantern and then lay next to her. Her body is covered by the blanket. I rest my hand on her waist to pull her close. I am filled with shock by her naked skin. "When did you undress?", I say giggling.

"Why are you blushing?", she says laughing.

She makes me feel so alive. My cheeks and ribs hurt from laughing with her everyday. She makes me feel confident and strong. I never have to question myself because she reasures me before I can. She is my best friend.

She places a single kiss on my lips and then looks up at me. I place my lips back on hers. I move on top of her. I need to be closer to her.

I capture her mouth with so much need to taste her. I remove my lips for hers and place tiny kisses down her body. With each moan I move faster. I finally get to the spot that she wants me at most. Her groans grow louder and louder with every stroke of my tongue. I love listening to her come undone. I sit up to remove my pants.

She then stands up and drags a blanket and sleeping bag along with her as she leaves the tent. I quickly follow behind her. Amelia lays the blanket out on the ground.

Her body has never looked more perfect than it does right now. The moon highlights every curve. She gestures for me as she lays down on the blanket. My fingers move across her body the moment I lay next to her. I run my finger tips down her arm back and forth. I get lost in the feeling of her soft skin and the goosebumps covering her body.

Our lips crash together with heat that feels like a flame ready to ignite as I climb on top of her. I move inside her slowly. I catch the moan escaping her with my mouth. I move all the way inside her as she wraps her arms around my neck. We both exhale at the same time.

I look deep into her eyes. Her face lets me know she is in just as much bliss as I am in.

Our lips find each other with desperation. My tongue enters her mouth. I explore her mouth needing to taste every inch. I start moving faster and faster. I love the sound of her falling apart beneath me. I am losing myself with each movement. Her saying my name is causing me to lose any bit of control I still have. I can tell she is about to come undone. I grab hold of her and move faster.

I can still feel the heat from our bodies despite the cool night breeze. I am lost in the smell of her hair, her hands in my hair, and the feeling of how wet she is.

Our bodies are one, moving effortlessly in the moonlight. We finish together, falling back onto the blanket. The sound of our heavy breathing is all I can hear.

I finally catch my breath and look over at her. She is looking up at the sky. The stars are beautiful, but nothing compares to her. "You are the most beautiful thing I have ever seen, Amelia.", I whisper.

She rolls over and buries her face into my chest. I look up at the sky and wonder what I did to deserve so much happiness.

I wrap Amelia up in the blanket and carry her into the tent. After I turn off all the lanterns I pull her into my arms. I fall asleep listening to the sound of her breathing.

Chapter Fifteen

Amelia

I wake up dizzy and confused.. I sit up to look around. "Amelia, I am so glad you are awake you had us all worried."Colin says frantically.

His face is pale and full of worry and distress.

We are all in a big dark room. I am taking a mental tally of everyone. Everyone is here except Troy.

"What is going on I ask", panicking.

Everyone looks sad and worried. "I think we were all taken last night", Stella says, trying to stay calm.

"Taken? Taken by who?", I say, but then I know exactly who took us. The Serpents.

"I think someone betrayed us", Blaze says.

"You do not know that!". Hannah screams out, her voice filled with so much pain.

"I do not want to believe it either, Hannah. But it is what it looks like.", Amber says, her eyes red and swollen from crying.

"We have to get out of here! Grandmother is going to come looking for us. This is going to be a trap if we do not help her!", I yell.

"We are trying to come up with a plan, honey. This room is locked with a spell from the outside. We have all tried to break it but we have not succeeded.", my mother says.

Everyone looks defeated. "How long have I been asleep? When did you guys wake up?" I ask.

"We have been awake for at least three hours. We tried to wake you but you wouldn't budge." Colin says.

We all jump at the sound of something at the door and run into a corner together. My grandfather stands in front of us all, ready to attack.

A woman with a hood over her head creeps in. She whispers a spell as she shuts the door.

She pulls her hood over her head to reveal her face. "I am not here to harm any of you. I am here to give you all a message.", she says.

She is a small woman with short, curly, and gray hair. Her eyes are an orange color.

We move closer to her, ready to listen. "My name is Penelope. I have been Ethan's servant for many years. Ethan's wife's name was Valerie. She was lovely. She was not meant to get pregnant let alone be his wife. He was so cruel to her. Even when she carried his child he showed her no mercy or compassion. We became very close while she lived here. One day when I was about to bring Ethan his dinner I overheard him tell one of his guards that he was going to have Valere murdered the moment she gave birth. I was devastated. I came up with a plan with a few servants I knew I could trust to save Valerie. Once their son was born we acted like she passed away during childbirth. She escaped without us knowing where so that way no one but her would ever know. At least that's what I thought. Then one day Adam asked what really happened to his mother. He had seen the cruelty that his father caused. I told him the truth. He was sixteen at the time. I knew he was planning something big. He was focused on finding her. He hid what he was doing by being dedicated to Ethan at the same time. Then a couple years later he told me goodnight. I could tell from the look in his eyes that he had found her. I begged him to tell me. He said that he found this couple that was going to help him die. I was appalled.

But he laughed, saying it was only going to look like he died. The next day he was going to battle this couple with other serpents and when everyone was distracted they were going to cast a spell to make him go into a coma.

He knew that Ethan never really cared for him. Ethan did exactly what he knew he would do. He told the guards to leave Adam there. He said Adam had disappointed him. After the serpents had left, the couple took him to his mom. I have not heard from him since then. Until two days ago.

"The couple was my parents. Weren't they," Colin whispers.

Everyone is so quiet.

"Yes. It was your parents.", Penelope says.

Seth kicks the wall causing all of us to jump. Grace wraps her arms around him. Tears are falling down her face.

I feel my heart breaking. I cannot imagine how Colin is feeling right now. He must be relieved in some way that he knows the truth. But he must be devastated that they died carrying that big of a secret.

"Why did Adam contact you two days ago?", my grandfather asks.

"Valerie got a message from your wife. She had a vision of her and Adam together. She knew he was still alive. She wanted to meet with them.", Penelope answers.

"Meet with them about what?", my grandfather says.

"I am not sure. I have not heard from them since.", she answers.

"How did you know we would be here?", I ask.

"Unfortunately the rest of the staff heard about the plan to take you guys. Ethan had an agent of his own helping him take you guys down.", she says quietly.

"What is his name?", Amber says, her voice cracking.

"Troy.", Penelope answers.

Amber moves over to Hannah. She holds her as they both cry. I never thought I would see Hannah so broken.

"How long has he been working with Ethan?", I ask.

"He has been a Serpent for two years.", Penelope answers.

Hannah gasps. Their cries grow louder. "How could I have been so stupid?", she yells.

"I am so sorry, but we have to leave right now. I have to get you guys past the gate. Once you are past the gate you can wait for Elenor." Penelope says.

We all head towards the door. Blaze helps Amber and Hannah to their feet. The brokenness on their faces is heartbreaking.

I wrap my arms around my parents and Colin. I feel like we are all in shock. Joseph and Kate died with Adam's secret. They saved his life.

They knew all these years that he and his mother were alive. We all knew they were heroes. But we never knew really how far they would go to do the right thing. They inspire me everyday. I am going into this battle with their strength and good heart.

"Today we are going to be Joseph and Kate. We are fighting for good. No matter the cost. They did not die for nothing, but they also never expected anything in return. I believe in every single one of you. Just as much as I believe in Colin's parents. We are in this together.", I say.

Everyone shakes their heads in agreement. I can see the confidence in all their faces. We can do this.

I grab Colin's hand as Penelope opens the door.

Chapter Sixteen

Colin

The way to the gate is fast through the servant passageway. It leads right down to the basement and then outside. Before we know it the gate is within eyesight.

"This is where I must leave you guys. I hope you guys succeed. I have seen such terrible things. All of this should have ended a long time ago.", Penelope says in a sad voice.

She walks back into the basement. We all turn towards the gate. "We are going to make a run for it. If you know how to do a cloaking spell, cloak as many people as you can. Remember, we just have to make it past the gate.", Seth says.

Everyone squeezes together. Blaze, Chelsea, Xavier, Seth, Grace, Hannah, Rick, and Jack cloak all of us.

"Stay together. Do not make any sudden movements. Link arms with the person next to you. Once we're out of the gate we can run to safety.", Blaze says.

We all start walking together. Amelia is holding on to my arm and Stella is on the other side of her.

Our steps are so slow. I do not think any of us are even blinking or breathing. We are approaching the gate. I feel the relief swelling up inside me. I just want to get everyone out of here safely.

My heart is pounding. I can feel Amelia's body shaking next to me. It kills me knowing how afraid she is.

All of a sudden a thunderous bursting sound comes from the sky!

A giant tree shatters right in front of us. We are all jolted apart. The cloaks are down. We are all vulnerable and in danger.

Ethan comes flying down to the gate carrying something. He lands with a sadistic laugh.

Finally I can see what he's holding. It is Penelops hood. Blood is dripping from it onto the ground.

Amelia and Stella gasp then break down into tears at the same time.

Everyone is filled with rage and sadness. Another person, selfishly killed.

"All that I could get out of her was that she helped you guys escape. But I still do not know why she helped you all. Anyone want to speak up?", Ethan asks angrily.

We are all silent.

"Well anyone? It was important enough for her to die over? What is it?" Ethan yells.

"We are not going to tell you anything.", Hannah says sternly.

Leah links her arm around Hannah's," Yeah we are not going to tell you anything."

We all link our arms together again. We are a team. We will fight right now before we submit to him.

"Are you mad that my soldier fooled you into falling for him?"Ethan says to Hannah.

"You are a coward! You make children do your dirty work for you!"Grace yells at Ethan.

"We are not afraid of you. We would rather die than submit to you!"Chelsea yells.

"Well, if death is what you want, then death you shall have.", He says, then snaps his fingers.

A hoard of serpents start coming from every direction. We are surrounded.

I look at Amelia one last time before I let go. I pull out my wand and begin to fight.

With every Serpent I take down five more come out. I try to keep an eye on Amelia but there is just too much commotion. The sweat is pouring down my face.

The ground is shaking from Wesley blowing things up. Serpents are flying through the air.

Zeke is making the serpents go unconscious by using his mind control spells.

Amelia is launching boulders and rocks. Alice goes up into the sky with each boulder she throws. While in the sky Alice shoots out shards of ice.

Wyatt is freezing serpents that are coming to buy us some time.

I want to help everyone but I can't. Blaze is going after Ethan. He is getting closer to him. Seth, Jack, Ace, and Rick are right behind him.

Grace and Carol are trying to heal people as they go. They can barely keep up.

Leah and Hannah are working together by throwing fireballs. The ground is covered in flames and the air around us is filling up with smoke.

Everyone else is fighting as many serpents as they can.

All of sudden I am being attacked. There are ten of them. Each one has the same evil look in their eyes. They are all different ages. Some are my age, older, and even younger.

They are not holding back. I cast out a spell causing a few of them to launch up into the sky.

Reid and Martin come to help me. As soon as we defeat them I look up to see Mia, the Serpent Amelia told me about. She is headed right towards Amelia.

I start running towards them as fast as I can.

Then everyone stops. I come barreling into Jack. We both stumble until we regain our balance.

Even the serpents stop moving.

I look over to see what everyone is staring at.

There are three people in hoods standing outside of the gate. Ethan is starting right at them.

The one in the middle removes their hood. It is Elenor. Nobody moves.

The one on the left removes their hood. It is Adam. Nobody moves.

I look at Ethan. His face and eyes are bright red. Electricity is coming out of his hands.

The one on the right removes their hood. It is Valerie. Adam looks just like her.

They both have auburn hair. Valerie's is long. Adam's is short. Their eyes are both a beautiful shade of honey.

Ethan screams out so loud that the ground, trees, and everything else shakes.

"How dare you!"Ethan screams at Elenor. It is clear that all of his rage is directed towards her.

But she does not look afraid.

"Enough is enough. It does not have to be this way!"Adam yells at Ethan.

"Do not speak to me. You were never my son. You were just a disappointment. A MISTAKE!"Ethan yells back.

Valerie puts both hands together and shoots a fireball right at Ethan. He barely blocks it. "You will never hurt us again.", she says defiantly.

The serpents look at Ethan. He nods his head with a violent and sick look in his eye.

Everyone goes back to battling. My eyes dart back towards where Mia was before. But she is no longer there. I then spot Amelia helping Hannah and Leah.

They are freezing large logs and throwing them into groups of serpents. When they reach the ground they shatter, sending shards from every direction.

Blaze, Rick, and Seth are headed towards Valerie and Adam.

Elenor is fighting Ethan. Alone.

No one is stepping in or helping.

I start helping Ace and Wyatt. We send waves of water into the crowd causing the serpents to be washed away. Some of them have even started to retreat back. Wesley is doing really well at keeping anymore serpents from coming in. All you can see is dirt, grass, and pieces of the ground bursting around him.

I look back at Amelia. She is so powerful. I just wish she wasn't so far away. As soon as the thought crosses my mind my eyes fall on Mia. She is sneaking up behind Amelia.

I scream out but Amelia cannot hear me. The explosions are deafening. It is too loud and I am too far away. I am running as fast as I possibly can. Mia has her wand in the air.

I cannot breathe. I cannot lose her. It feels like the world around me is silent and moving in slow motion. My feet won't move fast enough. I keep screaming, but no one can hear me.

Stella jumps in front of her right as the spell leaves Mia's wand.

Stella crashes to the ground.

Chapter Seventeen

Amelia

I turn around to Stella on the ground. Every ounce of life that I have leaves my body.

Mia takes off running. Her laugh echoes through the trees. Blaze and Seth chase after her.

I pull Stella into my arms. "Why? Why did you do that?"I scream.

The color in Stella's face is quickly fading.

"I promised I would have your back.", Stella whispers, wrapping her pinky around mine.

Then she takes her last breath in my arms. I pull her closer and hold her as tight as I can.

My whole body is shaking. I can feel my heart shattering into a million pieces. "Please! Please do not leave me! Please come back! I need you!", I scream out.

My throat feels like it is on fire from my screams.

Stella's parents fall to the ground in front of me. Her mothers hands tremble as she takes Stella from me.

Colin pulls me up and into his arms, but I have to keep going. He lets go, sensing my rage.

I do not look back at him. I attack everyone. I just start running and shooting off as many spells as I can. All I feel is hate and pain.

My grandmother sees Stella on the ground. Her face is riddled with anguish and sorrow. She is too distracted. Ethan raises his wand while her back is turned.

With all the rage, grief, pain, and despair I have swelling up inside me, I grab my Grandmother and shift out of the battle.

Everything is black, but I can still think.

I did not know it was possible for me to shift. I hadn't practiced at all.

I just knew I could not lose Stella and my grandmother at the same time.

I had to save her.

I keep screaming "Why?" as loud as I can,but the sound does not leave my mouth.

I want to cry, but tears do not leave my eyes. I feel empty, lost, and broken.

I wake up to my grandmother holding me. We are on the floor in my kitchen.

"Are you okay? How did I do that?", I ask.

"Pain is a very powerful emotion.", my grandmother says back, tears in her eyes.

But then she smiles. "What is it.?", I ask.

I feel one of her hands holding my head.

But then I notice her other hand.

It is resting on my stomach.

I feel the tears swelling up in my eyes.

"You are going to be a mother, Amelia."